ALSO BY AUDREY J. COLE

EMERALD CITY THRILLERS

THE RECIPIENT

INSPIRED BY MURDER

THE SUMMER NANNY: A Novella

VIABLE HOSTAGE

FATAL DECEPTION

BOOKS 1-5 BOX SET

STANDALONES

THE PILOT'S DAUGHTER

THE FINAL HUNT

ONLY ONE LIE

THE
ONE

AUDREY J.
COLE

RAINIER
PUBLISHING

The One
Copyright © 2023 Audrey J. Cole

ISBN: 978-1-7373607-7-3

Cover by Rainier Book Design
RainierBookDesign.com

Chapter 1

Sloane glances at the closed double doors of her home office as The One loads on her phone. She's still wearing her scrubs, having been too tired to change when she got home from the hospital. At forty-two, she's never used a dating app before. It feels weird, and not just because she's married.

She feels a tingle of apprehension as she taps the *JOIN NOW* button beneath The One's bold logo. Beneath it, in red, is their slogan: *Real connections. Lasting love.* Evelyn assured her after they finished stabilizing a gunshot victim earlier that night that The One wasn't like other dating apps. Her profile wouldn't be public and would only be seen by someone the data-driven app found as a *potential*.

"You just put in your age, gender, interests, and what you're looking for in a partner," Evelyn said, as Sloane washed her hands outside one of the ER's treatment rooms. "Then you take a short compatibility test. The app does everything else."

Sloane had heard of the app before, which was well-known for its success in using artificial intelligence to seemingly form real connections and long-lasting relationships. But she never thought she'd be using it. Then again, she also never thought Ethan would betray her.

"So, there's no photos?" Sloane stepped aside to make room for a trauma patient being transported to the OR.

Evelyn shook her head. "Not until The One finds your potentials. Then, after seeing their basic info, you can choose to message them and send a photo if you want. Or request one."

Sloane tossed a paper towel into the trash. "Sounds exhausting."

"Just think about it. It could be worth it, you know. It's how I met Ming."

"I took a few classes with Brody Carr in college. He was a premed major before he dropped out."

Evelyn's eyes widened. "You *did?*"

"We were chemistry lab partners for half a semester. He was really quiet and kind of a nerd. Not whom I would've expected to go on to create a billion-dollar dating app."

Evelyn raised her eyebrows. "Well, he doesn't seem nerdy now."

Outside, rain drums against the window behind where Sloane now sits in her favorite overstuffed chair. She pauses before answering the last question on the app's compatibility test. *How do you feel when you realize the person you are with is not the one for you?*

I feel shattered, she thinks as she stares at the multiple-choice options. But it's not one of the answers. For lack of a better option, she selects *I feel disappointed* and clicks *SUBMIT.* Hearts dance across the screen as the app searches for potentials.

"Hey."

Sloane jumps. Ethan stands in the doorway. She hates the feeling that she still gets when she sees him. That she still loves him, even after what he did.

"Sorry," he says, "I thought you heard me come in."

She presses her phone screen against her thigh, chiding herself for feeling guilty after what Ethan did. "I guess I didn't."

They hold each other's gaze in silence for a moment before Ethan speaks.

"What time is our appointment tomorrow?"

"Ten."

"Okay. I'll be in the guest room if you need me." He pauses, as if waiting for her to respond. "Good night," he finally says.

She waits until the door closes behind him before lifting her phone. *You have 5 potentials in your vicinity.* Below the message, a button flashes: *VIEW POTENTIALS.*

She taps her fingers against the armrest. *What am I doing?* Before she has time to change her mind, she closes out of the app and deletes it off her phone. A dating app isn't going to solve her marital problems. Hopefully, their couples counseling would.

After setting down her phone, she stares at the closed office doors. She bites her lip and grabs her phone from the armrest. She casts another glance at the closed doors before typing *Brody Carr* into the Internet search bar on her home screen.

❧

"It was a stupid mistake. I wish—"

Ethan's voice breaks, and Sloane turns her head to avoid his gaze, facing their marriage counselor, instead.

"I wish more than anything," he chokes, "that I could take it back."

Sloane tugs at the hem of her leather pencil skirt and shifts in the uncomfortable velvet chair.

Am I supposed to pity him? Feel empathy for the guilt he feels after sleeping with his homicide partner?

A burst of anger wells in her chest. They were supposed to be at the mountain lodge in the Cascades that she had booked for them, trying to get pregnant. Not here, listening to him recount how he slept with his partner during a weak moment following his father's death. *How could he have done this to me? To us?* Their therapist lifts her hand to her chin, watching Sloane.

Sloane looks out the window on the opposite side of the oversized office at the view of Elliot Bay, wondering if she should have gone into psychiatry instead of emergency medicine.

"I'm so sorry, Sloane. I know I don't deserve it, but please—I'm begging you to give me another chance."

She practiced telling him it was over in the bathroom mirror earlier this morning. She knows she was partly to blame for the issues in their marriage—before Ethan cheated. She prioritized the demands of her job, although the same could be said for Ethan.

She thinks of the five potentials generated by The One last night. She never even looked at them. The odds were good that at least one of them—if not all—could remain faithful, even when grieving the loss of a parent.

"Sloane, I love you. Please, let me prove it to you."

Out the corner of her eye, she sees Ethan swipe a tear off his cheek.

Their therapist sets her notepad on her lap. "It's up to you now, Sloane. Are you willing to forgive him?"

Sloane peers at Ethan's red pleading eyes, and the two-day stubble that covers his quivering chin. She would never have thought she could forgive infidelity. But he was so...broken.

And while he was the one who always wanted children, Sloane had come around to the idea.

"How am I ever supposed to trust him again?"

The therapist crosses her leg. "Rebuilding trust takes time. It's a choice. But it *can* be rebuilt."

Sloane exhales. She turns to Ethan, holding his gaze. How could she love and hate someone so much at the same time? She's never seen him look so scared. *But If I mattered so much to him, then why did he do this?* She tears her eyes away.

"What will you choose?" Their therapist folds her hands on top of her notepad while waiting for her answer.

Sloane knows what her mother would have done. She watched her mother stay despondently dependent on a string of unreliable men until she died. Whenever a relationship got too hard, her mother left in search of the next best thing—only to find another flawed man with different problems.

Sloane never planned to get married—until she met Ethan. She prided herself on believing what they had was different. But after Ethan cheated, Sloane understood better how her mother could so easily give up on a relationship. But Sloane refuses to allow her life to be thrown off course by a man's mistakes.

It would be easy for Ethan to have a child with someone else. But not for her. By the time they got divorced, and she found someone else she wanted to have a child with, it could be years. By that time, she might not be able to get pregnant, even with modern fertility treatments. Plus, she doesn't want to wait that long to become a mother. Even if she's able to get pregnant in her mid-forties, does she really want to be dropping her child off for kindergarten when she's fifty?

"Yes." She turns to Ethan. "At least, I'm willing to try."

What other choice does she have?

Chapter 2
Four Months Later

Sloane turns down the frozen food aisle at the Kirkland Market, a small organic grocer on the Lake Washington waterfront. She moves fast, knowing she doesn't have much time to shower and change before her and Ethan's seven o'clock dinner reservation. The chime of her text message alert interrupts Gwen Stefani's "Cool" that plays through the store's speakers. She spots the locally made huckleberry ice cream that Ethan loves and opens the freezer door before checking the message.

It was from Ethan. *Still working. Going to be late, probably around 8:30.*

She stops, staring at her phone until the screen goes dark. They'd hardly seen each other since their last couple's therapy appointment, thanks to both the hospital and police department being gravely understaffed. All the ER doctors were overworked, and it hadn't been easy to find someone willing to swap shifts so Sloane could have the night off. But Evelyn finally agreed.

She presses her lips together. When she agreed to try to forgive Ethan, she expected more of an effort on his part—not for things to go straight back to the way they were. Especially not tonight. Ethan knew she was ovulating. *Seems like the least he could do after screwing his partner.* As soon as she thinks it, their therapist's words play in her mind: *moving forward, always assume the best of each other.*

Sloane tosses the huckleberry ice cream into her basket. She types a reply, aware of someone moving slowly down the aisle in her direction. *Seriously? You said you would get the night off.* She's about to hit *Send* when a figure appears behind her in the reflection of the freezer door.

She whips around and steps aside, only to ram straight into the man's well-toned chest.

"Oh!" Her phone clamors to the floor.

She brings her hand over her heart as she reaches for it, but the man scoops it up seconds before her. Her hand touches his. She pulls it away as they stand.

"Sloane?" He holds out her phone.

She studies the attractive man standing in front of her.

"Brody?"

He grins, exposing his movie-star-white teeth. The dating app founder looks nothing like the lanky, shy guy she remembers from college. But she saw enough from her recent Internet search to know that after his success and fame from creating The One, he had changed.

"I'm so sorry," he says. "I didn't mean to sneak up on you like that."

She shakes her head. "It was my fault. I was...distracted."

He crosses his arms, making no effort to go his separate way. "Wow. You look...the same. In a good way."

Sloane feels herself smile. "I thought you lived in California now?"

"I did."

She glances at the gold wedding band on his left hand, recalling from her search that he'd married an Australian model.

"We did," he corrects, flashing his perfect white teeth again. "Just purchased a home up here. It's good to be back."

"Nice. In the city?"

"Medina, actually."

Of course. Medina was home to some of the wealthiest people in the country.

"What are you doing these days? Did you go on to medical school?"

She nods, impressed at his recollection. "I did. Even though my lab partner bailed on me halfway through my first semester of chemistry."

He grins, catching the playfulness in her tone.

"I'm an ER doctor now, at Bayside."

"Wow." He folds his arms. "Although, I'm not surprised. You struck me as someone who would go on to great things."

"Thank you." She smiles at the compliment, wondering if it was genuine or if he was just a smooth talker.

"And you definitely didn't need me as your lab partner. I was cheating off you the whole time."

"I didn't notice."

He laughs. "Yes, you did."

"Okay, I did." She can't help but laugh, too. "You've done very well yourself. Did I read somewhere that your wife is a model?"

His smile fades. "Former model, yeah." He clears his throat. "I'd love to catch up sometime. If you want?"

"Oh." She nods. "Um...sure."

He motions toward her phone, still in her hand. "Do you mind? I'll put my number in."

She unlocks her phone before handing it to him. After a few swift moves of his thumbs, he gives it back.

"That was fast."

"I sent myself a text. You'll see it in your messages."

"Oh." She glances at her phone before dropping it into her purse. *Was that what people did these days?* "Okay."

"I'm really glad we bumped into each other. Let's talk soon." His eyes linger on hers before he slowly moves in the opposite direction.

Sloane turns for the front of the store, feeling a grin tug at the sides of her mouth. She heads toward the self-checkout and deletes the text she almost sent to Ethan before typing a new one. *No prob. I'll change the reservation to nine.*

∞

Sloane checks the clock on her nightstand when she steps out of her walk-in closet. She smooths the front of her new fitted black dress as she turns in front of her full-length mirror, forcing herself not to compare her reflection to Ethan's ex-homicide partner who transferred to another department after word got out about their one-night stand. The dress accentuates her slight curves perfectly, and she decides it was well worth the money. She needs Ethan to zip up the back, but he would be home any minute.

From her Edwardian home's second-story window, she spots headlights coming down her street. During the day, she had an unobstructed view of the Ballard Locks out her bedroom window. Now, lights twinkled from Ballard's hillside across the waterway.

Seeing the headlights pull into the driveway across the street, she steps away from the window, stifling her disappointment. Ethan's already ten minutes late. He's probably just stuck in traffic. If they leave in the next five minutes, they could still make it on time.

After leaving the Kirkland Market, she called the waterfront restaurant and was able to change their reservation to nine. Thankfully it was a Friday, and they were open late.

She tousles her short dark curls with her fingers before sitting on the end of her bed to slip into her Christian Louboutin pumps. Her phone pings on the bed beside her with another message. She sighs before lifting the phone, knowing Ethan was probably just now leaving the homicide unit. Which means they'd have to meet each other at the restaurant. And she would have to manage her zipper without him.

Won't be home til after midnight. Don't wait up. I got a break in a case. Sorry. Maybe we can try again next weekend?

Sloane tosses the phone onto the down comforter. Emotions battle inside her, anger and disappointment competing for first place. *Next weekend?* She'd be on nights. And no longer ovulating. Ethan knows this. Or, at least, he should.

They'd already put off trying for a baby after she found out about Ethan's affair. Now that she wants a child as much as Ethan does, he can't even come home.

She leans forward and cradles her face in her palms. Maybe she was a fool to give him a second chance. Why had Ethan put on such a show of emotions and begged her to stay if he didn't mean it?

She knows how dedicated he is to his work—and how understaffed they are—but she never minded until now. Of the two of them, *she's* always been the one obsessed with her career. The emergency room is understaffed too, but she still managed to get a night off. At this rate, they'd never have a baby. Or a relationship.

After kicking off her heels, she pads downstairs in her half-zipped thousand-dollar dress and pulls the huckleberry ice cream out of the freezer. With the pint in one hand and a spoon in the other, she sinks onto her white leather couch, not even bothering to turn on the lights. She's three bites in when a drop spills onto her dress, but she doesn't bother wiping it away. It's not like she would have another chance to wear it anytime soon.

The house is so quiet that she hears her phone chime from her upstairs bedroom. She licks the spoon and sets the ice cream on the coffee table before climbing the stairs. The marriage counselor's words play in her mind: *think the best of each other, not the worst.* Maybe it was Ethan saying he's coming home after all. Or at least sending a more heartfelt apology for missing their dinner.

When she gets to her room, she sees the text isn't from Ethan. It came from a number she doesn't recognize. *So great seeing you tonight, Sloane. You are as beautiful as ever. Brody*

Chapter 3

"Sloane?" Ethan closes the door to the garage.

The house is quiet as he moves through the spotless kitchen and living room. Sloane's hospital award gala wouldn't start for over an hour, but he wanted to make sure he was home in plenty of time for her big night.

"Sloane?" He stops at the base of the staircase, steeling himself before he faces her.

He glances at the bouquet of peach roses in his hand. After he missed their anniversary dinner a month ago, Sloane told him she needed space. But now, she seems to resent him giving it to her.

She's hardly spoken to him since, not seeming to understand it was out of his control. He planned to have the night off until hours before their dinner reservation when he located the prime suspect in a recent hit-and-run that killed a thirty-six-year-old mother of two. When he discovered the suspected driver had been hiding out in a friend's Tacoma apartment, he had no choice but to make the arrest alongside his partner and a SWAT team. By the time they finished booking him, it was well past midnight.

He brought her a pumpkin spice latte at work a couple of times in the last few weeks. But both times was told by one of the nurses that

Sloane was too busy to see him, so he'd left her coffee at the front desk.

He starts up the stairs. Tonight will be different. His new partner is covering for him, and Ethan booked them a suite at the historic downtown hotel where they spent their wedding night. He isn't even taking his work phone with him, so they will be sure to be uninterrupted.

He hears her voice when he gets to their bedroom, but the room is empty. A giggle erupts from behind the closed door to their en suite bathroom. It's been so long since he's heard her laugh like that, it sounds almost foreign. He knows he should announce himself, but instead he finds himself creeping past their made bed.

"I have to go," Sloane says. "Ethan will be home soon."

Ethan stares at the closed bathroom door. Hearing the decidedly male voice come through Sloane's phone speaker, he feels the hairs stick up on the back of his neck.

"I wish you could be there tonight, too." Her tone is hushed. "Oh, stop!" She laughs again.

Ethan takes a few steps back as her voice nears the bathroom door.

"Thanks, Brody. I'll let you know how it goes."

When the door opens, Ethan is standing beside their bed. She's wearing a short satin robe and more makeup than usual. The light in Sloane's eyes dims when she sees him. It's the same look she's given him countless times since she learned of his affair. A reminder of what a raging disappointment he is to her. His father looked at him the same way after Ethan told him he was becoming a cop.

"Ethan. You're home early."

Her eyes fall to the flowers in his hand.

"I wanted to make sure I got here in plenty of time." He extends the bouquet toward her. "I'm so proud of you."

She accepts the flowers, but her smile looks forced.

"Who were you talking to?"

"*Hmm?*" She sniffs the bouquet before setting it on the bed.

"In the bathroom." Ethan tries to stifle the jealousy that surges in his chest.

"Oh." She turns her back to him and strides toward the walk-in closet, phone still in hand.

Ethan follows behind her, getting a whiff of a fruity perfume he's never smelled before.

"I was just practicing my acceptance speech for tonight."

She starts to untie her robe as she shuts the closet door behind her. Ethan presses his palm against the wall beside the doorway, fighting the urge to fling open the door and demand to know who she was talking to.

Instead, he turns and sinks onto the end of the bed. She hates him. He can see it in her eyes. And he doesn't blame her after what he did. But the last thing he expected was for her to seek comfort in another man. Maybe he was a fool to not consider this possibility. *Some detective I am if I couldn't see this coming.*

He flexes his jaw, hearing her humming from inside the closet. She says she's forgiven him. But she hasn't. And she won't. Not until she can understand what it's like to make a stupid mistake. She's achieved so much, and without help from anyone, that she's forgotten what it's like to be human. Driven herself to perfection.

Lately, he's wondered if he'd be better off with someone else. A woman with hobbies instead of an all-encompassing, high-performance profession. One who loves Christmas and children. A woman whose perfectionism doesn't illuminate all his own flaws. But he loves Sloane. Her drive, intellect, and beauty are incomparable to anyone else. Coming so close to losing her has made him realize it more than ever. And he's not ready to give up.

He thinks of what she told the man on the phone. *I wish you could be there tonight, too.*

A lot of her physician coworkers were likely attending the gala. *So, who is this guy? How did they meet?*

Ethan looks at the roses lying beside him. They aren't enough. Neither is the hotel he booked tonight. Nothing will ever be enough until Sloane can grasp what it's like to be flawed.

Chapter 4

S loane slides her black dress out of the dry-cleaning bag, glad to see the huckleberry ice cream stain is gone. She smiles, thinking of Brody jokingly asking her if she was prepared to face the paparazzi after being named Doctor of the Year before he turned serious. *I'm rooting for you. Even though I can't be there.*

She wonders what's going through Ethan's head on the other side of her closet door. While the geek turned billionaire had an unexpected sense of humor, no one could ever make her laugh like Ethan used to. In the first few years of their relationship, there were times Ethan made her laugh so hard she fell on the floor. Now, she can't even remember the last time Ethan made her laugh like that.

She and Brody had been exchanging texts for only a week when he asked her to coffee during a rare afternoon lull in the ER. The two of them stayed for nearly an hour at the northwest-themed coffee shop next to the hospital. It felt like they just sat down when Sloane checked her watch, shocked to see the time.

"Well, you're in a good mood today," Evelyn said to her later, after they stabilized two trauma victims who'd arrived by ambulance after a head-on collision.

Sloane realized she'd been grinning as she peeled off her bloody gloves and disposable gown. A week later Brody asked her to coffee again, and she managed to sneak away for a half hour despite a hectic shift. He opened up about his recent separation from his wife, which they were keeping out of the news for now, knowing what it might do to the stock of his company once the word was out.

Her phone pings as she steps into the dress. It's a text from Brody. *You sound great. Knock 'em dead tonight.* She bites her lower lip as another smile reaches her lips.

"Sloane?"

She sets down her phone at the sound of Ethan's voice. She slips her arm through the strap of her dress and opens the closet door.

Ethan stands at the foot of their bed. He's reholstered his gun since she came out of the bathroom. Her smile fades at the hard expression on his face.

"What is it?"

"I have to go back to work."

"*What?*"

He can't be serious.

She searches his gray-blue eyes, waiting for him to laugh and say he's kidding. But he doesn't.

He gestures to the phone in his hand. "I just got a text from Jonah. The prosecutor has called a meeting about our hit-and-run case. There's been some new evidence. I'm so sorry, Sloane."

"What new evidence? You said Jonah was covering for you."

Ethan shakes his head. "He was. But I can't miss this meeting." He takes a step toward her. "I need to go."

Her jaw falls open as Ethan kisses her forehead. *Unbelievable.* He is already making for their bedroom door by the time words reach her mouth.

"Wait! You promised me! There has to be someone else. Tell them you can't."

He turns when he reaches the doorway. He does look pained, she'll give him that. But it's not enough to quell the anger forming inside her.

"Don't wait up. I'll be home late."

Sloane feels her chest heave. She's tempted to remind him what an important night this is for her. And that he owes her one. What her coworkers will say when she attends the ceremony alone. *Could he not just give me this one night?*

Looking into his eyes, she decides it's not worth it. She knows him well enough. She won't change his mind. She used to respect that he gave his all to his work...before he slept with his partner.

She clenches her hands into fists as he disappears down the hall. "Ethan!" she hears herself shout.

"I'm sorry. I can't miss this meeting," he calls from the stairs.

Sloane stands still as she hears the front door open.

"I'm proud of you, Sloane. I know you'll be great."

She stares at the roses on her bed as the front door closes, wanting to throw them across the room. Instead, she paces back and forth on the plush carpet.

Being awarded Doctor of the Year by the largest trauma center in the Pacific Northwest was a huge achievement, even for Sloane. *How dare he back out on me tonight?* Why had she gone to the trouble of forgiving him if he wasn't even going to *try?*

She stops pacing and swears, realizing she now has no one to zip up her dress. With shaking hands, she reaches behind her back. After five minutes of sucking in and bending backwards at awkward angles, she manages to pull the zipper to the top.

Her breathing has calmed when she heads back to her closet to retrieve her phone and shoes. On her way out, she catches her reflection in the mirror and sighs. When Ethan overheard her bathroom phone call with Brody, she expected him to give a damn. Not to abandon her on the most important night of her career without even putting up a fight.

∞

Sloane downs her second glass of Chardonnay, now that her acceptance speech is over. Beside her, Evelyn giggles at something her doting stay-at-home husband whispers into her ear.

"I hope he knows what he's missing," Evelyn said when Sloane arrived at the gala alone. "You could do so much better, Sloane. If you ever decide to leave him, Ming's best friend is newly single and I also know a few really great guys. But they won't be single forever."

Sloane looks beyond her glass award plaque at the empty seat next to her. Before leaving the house, she thought about inviting Brody. Maybe *that* would get Ethan's attention. But she decided against it. Brody made it clear that the public couldn't yet know about the status of his marriage.

Evelyn leans into Sloane, following her gaze. "I don't understand why you don't leave him already. It's not like the two of you have children."

The words slice like a scalpel at Sloane's heart. She pulls out her phone as the hospital director steps up to the stage and begins his drawn-out closing remarks.

There's a new text from Brody. *How did it go, rockstar? Wish I could've seen you win that award tonight.*

She stares at her phone as Evelyn laughs loudly at the director's lame attempt at a joke. *Ass kisser.* Despite the smile that forms on her lips after reading Brody's text, she feels a crush of disappointment to see there are none from Ethan.

He couldn't help it, she reminds herself. She knows the demands of Ethan's job aren't his fault and has always respected his commitment to the cause. *But why can't he apply that level of commitment to me?*

Is he ever going to confront her about the phone call?

She's debating how to reply to Brody when Evelyn elbows her. She turns to see her coworker giving her a pursed-lip look, as if to say *Get off your phone. The director's watching.*

But for once, Sloane couldn't care less about schmoozing with the medical director, even though she has ambitions of becoming the director herself one day.

If Ethan can't come through for her on one of the proudest moments of her career, something has to be done. Ignoring Evelyn's look of warning, Sloane types her response.

The banquet is almost over. I really want to see you tonight.

Sloane joins in the applause as the director steps down from the podium, having no idea what he said, only glad it's over. On the table, her phone lights up with a text from Brody. Sloane taps the screen to see the full message. *I'd love that. I'm out on my patio enjoying the city lights. Want to meet somewhere?*

Evelyn stands and places a hand on Sloane's shoulder. "The director's coming over. You might want to get off your phone."

Sloane follows Evelyn's gaze, spotting the director making his way through the crowd from across the room, stopping to greet nearly every attendee along the way. Sloane types a quick reply to Brody. *How about I come to you? Those city lights sound nice.*

"Congratulations, Dr. Marks."

Sloane turns and accepts the handshake from one of the hospital's board of trustees. "Thank you."

Her phone illuminates when Brody replies with his address.

The director nearly reaches them when Sloane pushes back her chair. She scoops up her award and phone from the table. "See you tomorrow."

Evelyn's eyes dart toward the director before staring at Sloane. "You can't leave yet."

Sloane feels the director's eyes on her as she stands. "I have to go. I'll see you in the morning."

"Sloane—"

She slips into the crowd and leaves the banquet hall without looking back, hearing Evelyn's tone morph into pleasantries as the director approaches.

Chapter 5

Jonah looks up from a case file with surprise when Ethan strides into their cubicle. "I thought you were going to that award dinner with your wife?"

Ethan moves past his partner and takes a seat at his desk. "Turns out she didn't need me to go." Sloane's giddy laughter replays in his head.

"Oh." Jonah closes the file and swivels in his chair. "Everything okay?"

"Yeah." Ethan clears his throat, coming to terms with his decision. "Fine."

The hospital's gala would have started by now, and he can only imagine what's going through Sloane's head as she sits next to his empty seat, waiting to receive her award. A sinking feeling forms in his stomach as he opens his laptop. Maybe he was wrong to think that pushing her farther into another man's arms could be the thing that saves their marriage.

"All right." Jonah swivels back to face his desk when Ethan doesn't elaborate.

Ethan opens his email, relieved when his partner doesn't push for any more explanation.

"Can't say I mind having the help. I got a new shooting about an hour ago. The victim's in surgery."

Ethan's partner is still new to the department, having been hired to replace Rachel after news spread of their affair and she transferred to the intelligence unit. While Jonah is competent, Ethan finds himself missing his more seasoned partner from time to time. Although, it's his own fault they aren't working together anymore.

Everything lately seems to be his fault.

Ethan stares at his inbox, unable to concentrate on anything besides Sloane's hushed words in the bathroom. *Thanks, Brody. I'll let you know how it goes.* Who is this guy?

He opens an email, pretending to read. Maybe he should have put up a fight. Showed Sloane that he loves her and can't stand the thought of her being with someone else. He glances at the time in the corner of his laptop screen. If he leaves now, he'd only be a few minutes late to her award ceremony.

He chews his lip. But that wouldn't fix anything. Not really.

He can't bear the resentment in Sloane's eyes every time he comes through the door. He wants his wife back, and what they had together, not just a shell of what they once were.

If she makes the same mistake that he did, maybe there will be something different in her eyes. Understanding. Forgiveness.

"I've got a couple of people still to interview for our new homicide. You want to come?"

Ethan spins in his chair. "Which one?"

In the last two weeks, they had gotten two new homicide cases.

"Steven Knox."

"Ah."

They already had the victim's thirty-five-year-old son with no criminal history in custody after charging him with the shooting death of his father during a late-night altercation. But, as usual, they still had some loose ends to tie up.

Jonah rocks back and forth in his swivel chair. "It's so messed up. I can't even imagine ever laying a hand on my old man. You know? Your *parent.*"

"But my dad and I are pretty close," Jonah adds, filling the void of his partner's silence. "I guess everyone isn't so lucky."

Ethan recalls his father's reaction when he told him he was becoming a cop, instead of taking the bar exam after law school. When his dad all but wrote him off.

"You have a good relationship with your dad?"

"He passed earlier this year."

Jonah stops rocking. "I'm sorry."

"Thanks." Ethan stares at the edge of his desk. "He never liked me being a cop."

Jonah goes quiet, as if waiting for him to elaborate.

"He was a defense attorney. Thought all cops were crooked and power hungry. *And...*" Ethan sighs. "He eventually wanted me to take over his legal firm. But I had to go my own way. Couldn't spend my life living out someone else's dream, right?"

He vowed to be a good father if he ever got the chance. And he saw the toll running a law firm had taken on his dad—and their family. Ironically, he'd chosen a career that was just as demanding, if not more.

"No, you can't." Jonah stands and pulls on his coat. "Ready?"

"Yeah." Ethan closes his laptop, grateful for a distraction from second-guessing his move to bail on Sloane tonight.

Chapter 6

S loane's thoughts are consumed with Ethan as she drives across the floating bridge over Lake Washington. She slows beside the spotlights from the night construction crew, feeling like her impending indiscretion is on display for the world to see. She nearly smiles at the thought.

After taking the Medina exit, she follows her GPS through the exclusive lakefront community that is home to some of the world's richest tech entrepreneurs. She slows her Porsche to a stop in front of the gated entrance to Brody's waterfront home.

She's debating whether to press the button on the intercom when the gate rolls open. She takes a steadying breath and drives down the long winding road, passing a lit-up tennis court on her right before coming to a large circular drive. She stares up at the house without getting out of her car. The white two-story, L-shaped mansion accented with a black front door to match its dark windowpanes is even more opulent than she expected. Its flat roof and clean, square lines boast of its modern architecture.

Maybe I should go home. Ethan had already heard her on the phone with Brody, and it only managed to push him farther away. She puts her car in reverse just as Brody opens the front door. He's wearing jeans and a fitted polo shirt. Seeing him step out onto the front porch, Sloane throws her car into park and kills the engine.

Going home isn't the answer. Ethan needs to feel what she felt when he slept with his partner. He has to taste the fear of losing Sloane forever if things between them are to be mended.

"Wow," Brody says, as she strides across the stamped concrete. "You look amazing."

She climbs the steps to the sleek white porch. "Thank you."

Brody's muscular arms envelop her in a hug. She clings to him, lingering in his embrace before she pulls away.

He steps aside and motions for her to come in. She feels a strange feeling in her chest as she enters the mansion. It's the first time they have been alone together. She lifts her head to take in the two-tier, circular chandelier made from a translucent stone that hangs from the ceiling. It fills the starkly decorated space with a warm glow.

Brody claps his hands together. "I thought we could open a bottle of champagne to celebrate. This is a big night for you."

"That sounds great."

He leads her past a set of floating stairs with a glass railing. She feels another rush of nervous excitement. It's different from the bouts of adrenaline she sometimes feels working in the ER, when she has complete control.

He flashes her a playful smile and takes her hand, reminding her of the quiet, shy guy he was in college. *He's nervous,* she thinks. At least, he wants her to think he is. A guy like Brody Carr must be used to women swooning over him.

Comparing this moment to her first date with Ethan, she's struck by a bolt of sadness. The connection she shared with him was something that money couldn't buy. She had been immediately drawn to Ethan's humor, his drive, his empathy. To who he was. It never mattered what he *had*.

Where did we go so wrong?

They move past a blown-up underwater photograph on the wall. She slows to admire the bright red and yellow anemones and starfish, her mind whirling with thoughts of her husband. While she can appreciate being in a mansion, it's too bad money didn't equate to love.

"I took that," Brody says. "Freediving."

"You freedive?" She didn't know much about the sport aside from reading a news article a few years back about a freediver who died in a competition.

He nods. "When I can."

Sloane looks back at the bright sea life in the photograph, which had to have been taken on some tropical reef. "That's amazing."

They move side-by-side toward the rear of the house. She eyes a white grand piano.

"You play?"

"I do. Sometimes, classical. But mostly Radiohead."

She grins. "You're full of surprises, Brody Carr."

She stops when they reach an open-plan living room with a vaulted ceiling, seeing a framed photograph above the streaked-marble fireplace across the room. A diver in a hooded wetsuit swims parallel to a vertical rope beneath dark turquoise water. A smaller cable affixes the diver's ankle to the rope. The diver's pointed toes and arms at their side display a strong athleticism, and there is a strange tranquility to the photo. Above the photo, a gold medal hangs from a blue ribbon.

She turns to Brody. "You dove competitively?"

He shrugs. "A little. I enrolled in a freediving school in Florida after I dropped out of UW. I knew after taking those first few premed courses that college, and especially medical school, wasn't for me. I wanted to create something that would have an impact on the quality of people's lives. Freediving gave me a whole new perspective. On life. On everything."

She remembers him being such a loner in college. He always struck her as being awkward and timid. She can't imagine *that* guy enrolling in a freediving school. "You're not whom I expected you to be."

He lets out a short laugh as they cross the space, which is open to the outside, where flames flicker in an outdoor fireplace beneath a large covered patio. Beyond it, lights illuminate a swimming pool, and Seattle's city lights shine from the other side of the lake.

"Most people aren't." He lets go of her hand to effortlessly uncork the bottle of champagne sitting in a bucket of ice. "That's what gave me the idea for The One. We make false assumptions about people from the moment we see them. Many relationships fail because people pick partners who are wrong for them. People usually aren't who you think they are at first impression. When you meet someone new, it's easy to see what you want to see and be disappointed later when it turns out not to be true.

"The One eliminates that by using AI and statistical data to hone down your potentials to only people that you're truly compatible with. It's not foolproof, but if you're honest with the information you provide, you'll have over a ninety percent chance of compatibility with your potential matches."

Sloane wonders if the app would find her and Ethan compatible now. She's certain it would have when they first met ten years ago. Had they changed so much they were no longer right for each other?

She dismisses the doubt in her mind, refusing to accept it. It was what her mother used as an excuse to give up on one relationship after another. Fooling herself into thinking the grass was greener elsewhere, as soon as things got hard. Her never-ending search for a fairy tale kept her from seeing any relationship grow to fruition, because she was never willing to put in the work to make life what she wanted it to be.

She forces her attention back to the billionaire standing before her. "Your home is incredible."

"I'm glad you like it. *You're* incredible."

Brody hands her a glass before lifting his own. "To the Doctor of the Year."

Their glasses clink together. After they each take a sip, Brody takes her glass and sets them back on the table. He closes the space between them, and she takes in the cedar scent of his undoubtedly expensive cologne. He rests his hands on either side of her waist. She places her palms against his muscular chest. He leans forward, and their lips meet.

She wraps her arms around the back of his neck, noting the unfamiliar feel of his tongue exploring her mouth. She presses her body against his, wanting to embrace the moment. And push her cheating husband to the far corner of her mind. Everything about Brody feels unfamiliar. And she needs more.

A police siren sounds in the distance. *Ethan.*

She pulls away, breathing hard.

I've got to do this.

The playful look on Brody's face is replaced by one of longing. "Are you okay?"

He steps toward her, resting his forehead against hers. Sloane closes her eyes, feeling the rise and fall of his chest against hers.

The siren fades. Sloane forces herself to focus on Brody's hand moving through her hair before it slides down her arm, and he intertwines his fingers with hers. *Ethan didn't think of me before he slept with his coworker. Or did he?*

"I'm more than okay." She kisses Brody again before he steps back and leads her inside the house.

They move in silence through the first floor of the home until they come to a large bedroom, softly illuminated by a floor lamp in the opposite corner to the door. After leading her through the doorway, Brody turns and pulls her against him. He lifts her off the ground, pressing her back into the wall as she wraps her legs around him.

His mouth travels down her neck then returns to her lips. He steps back, setting her back on her feet. She lifts his shirt to the top of his chest, and Brody pulls it over his shoulders. She places her hands on his abs, pushing him toward the made bed in the middle of the room. His hazel eyes meld intently with hers, and she admires the sapphire ring around his irises.

As Brody unzips the back of her dress, her eyes catch on a large black-and-white photo on the wall.

"What's wrong?" His eyes follow her gaze as she stares at the nude silhouette.

Sloane recognizes Brody's wife from her photos online. It's the perfect excuse to leave.

"I should've taken that down. We *are* separated."

He places his hands on either side of her face and turns her head to face his. He lowers his mouth to hers. She pulls away.

"Please, don't be jealous."

"We can't do this." She backs away. "I have to go home."

"Please stay."

She steps out of his reach, shaking her head. "We're both married. I can't. I'm sorry."

"Sloane, wait!"

She moves into the hall without turning around. She hears Brody call her name again as she finds her way to the front door. But she doesn't stop.

She inhales the cool October air when she steps outside. As she marches toward her Porsche, she feels a chill up her back. Feeling behind her, she remembers Brody unzipping her dress. But she isn't about to stand in his driveway for the ten minutes it would likely take for her to get it zipped back up.

She looks back at the mansion as Brody appears on the front porch.

"Please," he calls. "I'm sorry. We can take it slow."

"Good night, Brody."

She smiles to herself when she climbs behind the wheel at the look of longing on the rich app founder's face. Tonight wouldn't be enough to right the ship of her broken marriage. But it was a start.

Chapter 7

E than waits until he hears the shower turn on in their master bathroom to sneak into the garage and check the GPS in Sloane's Porsche. He heard her come home last night not long after he went to bed. It was nearly midnight when he checked the clock. Much too late for her to have come straight home after the award gala.

He tossed and turned all night, at one point nearly marching into their bedroom demanding to know who she'd been with after the ceremony. He was already awake that morning when her alarm went off across the hall, and it dawned on him that he could check her navigation history.

When he gets downstairs, he spots her purse on the kitchen counter. It takes him only a few seconds to find her key fob tucked inside the side pouch. Before opening the door to the garage, he pauses to make sure he can still hear water running upstairs.

He climbs in sideways when he gets to her Porsche, not wanting to adjust the seat. He turns on the car and drums his fingers against the wheel as he waits for her navigation screen to load. The map appears, and it takes him longer than he anticipated to find the most recent destination.

When the waterfront Medina address pops up, Ethan stares at the screen. Her time at the location was less than an hour. Medina was one of the most expensive zip codes in the country, and properties on the lake were worth upward of ten million dollars. He takes a photo of the address with his phone before turning off her car and going back inside.

The upstairs shower is still running. He drops her key fob into her purse and turns on the coffee pot, starting to feel relieved. Maybe he was wrong to think she'd sleep with someone else after he blew off her award dinner. A home like that had to belong to some major hospital donor. Maybe they had an after-party. Sloane was too ambitious not to attend, at least for a little while.

Rain beats against the kitchen window as he pours a cup of coffee, not waiting for the full pot to brew. What was he thinking last night? Pushing Sloane into someone else's arms would only bring catastrophe. He wonders if a part of him wanted her to cheat as a way of feeling better for doing it to her.

He's starting to relax when he hears her footsteps on the stairs. Maybe he even misread the phone call he overheard yesterday. But he has to know the truth, or it's going to drive him crazy.

"Morning." Ethan leans against the counter, taking a sip of coffee as Sloane slams the refrigerator door after retrieving her almond milk.

She makes for her espresso machine and fires up the milk frother without answering. Ethan waits for the noise to stop before saying anything more, admiring her lean frame beneath her short silk robe as she finishes making her latte.

"How did it go last night?"

"Fine," she says without turning around.

"You got home late."

"I didn't know those things went so long," he adds when she doesn't respond. "Must've been quite the award ceremony."

She turns, latte in hand, looking him in the eye for the first time since coming into the kitchen. "It didn't. I went for a drink after with Evelyn and Ming."

He takes another sip from his mug. "Where'd you go?"

"A new cocktail bar downtown."

He's astonished at how good a liar she is. It's a little disturbing. She doesn't even blink.

He grips his mug tighter, trying not to let his emotions show. "*Hmm.* I thought maybe you went to an after-party or something."

She lets out a short laugh. "After-party? It wasn't the Super Bowl. Although maybe if I'd told you it was, you would've come."

She reaches into an upper cabinet for her pink Yeti, exposing her toned butt cheek. *Why is she lying about going to Medina?* Though he fears he already knows the answer. Otherwise, she would have told him the truth.

She marches past him after pouring her latte into her to-go mug. Ethan feels a surge of anger at her cold expression. She's not just cold, she also looks happy. After he slept with Rachel and realized the pain it would cause, he thought he might throw up. *She's not even sorry.*

Ethan raises his mug to his lips. "You're not really one to talk, you know. You've always put your career before me."

When they first met, Ethan was attracted to Sloane being a doctor. Maybe her drive and intelligence reminded him of his mother. But his mother has a heart. He's not sure now that the same can be said for his wife.

Sloane stops. "Because I *had* too. How do you think I got where I am? Not all of us grew up with rich, doting parents who made everything easy for them."

Ah, there it is. Her resentment is so palpable he can almost taste it. It was the reason he grew so close to Rachel after his dad died. Because she *cared*. Sloane's jealousy of Ethan's relationship with his dad—even though it was far from perfect—made her incapable of consoling him.

"Well, it sounds like you had a better time without me. You didn't want me there, and you know it."

Immediately, he regrets his words—and the disdain behind them—seeing the look on her face.

She narrows her eyes. "Excuse me? You think I *wanted* to go alone? Have my coworkers pity me, while I sat all night next to the empty seat meant for my cheating husband?"

Her words sting. "I'm sorr—"

"And don't act like you haven't put your career first, too," she adds. "I'm home more than you are."

Ethan shakes his head. "Only because we are so short-staffed right now. But you put off having children so long, who knows if we even can, still? You *knew* I wanted a family. And you made me think you did too."

But Sloane was never interested in having children until her female colleagues started having them while balancing their careers, making Sloane feel they one-upped her.

"All you care about is proving you don't need anyone. Congratulations, you've succeeded." He sucks in a breath, again hating his words but also feeling powerless to stop them coming out.

Her face flushes with color. He's seen that look before—she's infuriated.

"Are you seriously putting the fact we don't have children on *me*? The only reason I'm not pregnant right now is because you *cheated* on me!" She yells the last part loud enough for the neighbors to hear.

Ethan stares into his coffee. "I've never been good enough for you."

She scoffs. "Stop acting like I'm your father, Ethan. I'm your *wife*." Her last word comes out a hiss.

My wife who doesn't even feel guilty after sleeping with someone else.

Sloane takes a few steps toward him. "How dare you blame me for what *you* did." She whips around. "You're unbelievable," she shouts before storming up the stairs.

Ethan wants to go after her, but he can't think of anything to say that wouldn't make things worse. She hates him. Part of him hates himself too. He was wrong. He should've gone with her last night.

He's still leaning against the kitchen counter ten minutes later when Sloane comes back, dressed in scrubs. She snatches her purse off the counter without even a glance in his direction and slams the door to the garage behind her.

Chapter 8

"**I** don't understand—" The man's voice breaks. "What happened?"

Sloane gives the man she just introduced herself to a moment to collect himself in the small room off the ER waiting room.

"I'm sorry, I didn't get your name?" Sloane asks.

"Daniel."

The woman seated beside him reaches for his hand.

"This is my sister, Janae."

Janae grasps her brother's hand as Daniel wipes his eyes with a tissue. Sloane had already pronounced Daniel's forty-eight-year-old wife dead when he and his sister arrived at the ER. The siblings don't look much older than Sloane.

Daniel refocuses his attention on Sloane, shock and grief in his eyes. Sloane has seen this look countless times over in her career. But while it's familiar, it still moves her every time. A reminder that, sometimes, our love for others comes at a cost.

"She was fine this morning. We were in the middle of a conversation when she..." His chin quivers. "Stopped answering me and collapsed on the kitchen floor."

"We've ruled out a heart attack, but we'll have to wait for the autopsy to determine what caused her death." Sloane guessed it was either a pulmonary embolism or an aneurysm. "I'm sorry we don't have more answers at the moment."

"Can I see her?"

"Of course." Sloane stands and leads them down the busy ER corridor to the room where his wife's body remains, after they were unable to resuscitate her.

After answering all the questions she can, Sloane steps out into the hall, leaving Daniel and his sister in the hands of a nurse and a chaplain. She pulls off her mask and inhales a deep breath as she moves down the vacant corridor toward the staff breakroom. Her mouth feels dry. She can't remember the last time she took a drink of water or peed.

How would Ethan look if she died today? She thinks of his cutting words this morning. *Will we even still be together when one of us dies?*

When she got into her car after her argument with Ethan, she checked the search history on her navigation. Brody's address came to the top, which confirmed Ethan *had* overheard her on the phone with Brody. She knew he wasn't asleep when she got home last night, much too late to have come home straight after the gala. She left her key fob visible at the top of her purse, knowing he would check to see where she'd been.

She remembers telling Ethan once that she went to college with the app founder and has no doubt her homicide detective husband will look up the homeowner of the Medina address. It wouldn't be long before he put it together. She imagines the look on Ethan's face when he figures out that she went to the billionaire app founder's home after he backed out of her award gala.

Before now, Ethan had no idea what it feels like to suffer when the one you love violates your trust. He's never had to worry about that with Sloane. She doubts he even thinks—after everything—she has it in her to cheat.

She pushes open the breakroom door, surprised to hear laughter after the shift they've had. Although, most of them only had two hours to go, so maybe euphoria is setting in.

"Congratulations," Logan says, as he moves past Evelyn.

Evelyn is beaming when she looks up from her seat, despite them just losing their fifth patient of the day. "Thanks, Logan."

Sloane steps aside for Logan to pass through the doorway. "Nice job earlier."

She's grateful he wasn't among the nurses who called out sick today. Logan had been working there longer than Sloane, and she could count on him to anticipate what she needed before she asked.

"You too." Logan sighs, looking at his watch. "Two more peaceful hours."

Logan disappears down the hall, and Sloane turns toward Evelyn as she makes for the watercooler.

"Congratulations for what?"

"I wanted to tell you first, but there was no time between patients this morning. Then Logan caught me throwing up in a waste basket in one of the empty treatment rooms when I couldn't make it to the bathroom. I'm pregnant."

Sloane stops. "Oh! That's great! I didn't know you and Ming were trying." She tries to remember how old Evelyn's twins are. They can't be more than two.

"Well, we weren't exactly *trying*. But we're ecstatic just the same." She lets out a lighthearted laugh. "You should've seen Ming's face when I told him. I wish I would've videoed it. He's so excited."

A heaviness forms inside Sloane's chest as she feigns a smile. Evelyn is six years younger than her. Sloane was too career-focused in her thirties to consider children. Looking at Evelyn, she wonders if she should have done things differently. All she has to go home to after this crappy shift is an empty house.

Sloane turns to fill a cup with water as her smile turns into a frown.

"Ming says he's hoping it's a boy, but I know he also secretly wants another girl. We'll be thrilled either way. And it's just one this time—thank goodness!"

Sloane empties her water cup and fills it again as Evelyn carries on about how she's been even more nauseous with this pregnancy than she was with the twins. *What do I have, aside from this hospital? A husband who doesn't want to come home?*

But not for long, she reassures herself. That is all about to change. She trusts Ethan—at this very moment—is figuring out that he's on the brink of losing her, and not the other way around.

"Sorry." Evelyn stands from her seat as Sloane downs her second cup. "I didn't mean to go on about it." Evelyn steps toward her, crossing her arms. "How are things with Ethan? Weren't you guys going to start trying?"

Sloane wipes a drop of water off her chin with the back of her hand as Evelyn's eyes intently search hers. "They're great." She feels herself nod for extra emphasis. "We've just been working so much lately, I—"

She's cut off by the ringtone of Evelyn's hospital phone. Evelyn pulls her cell out of her scrub pocket.

"Dr. Long."

Evelyn lowers her gaze to the floor.

"What room?"

"Okay. I'm coming."

"And Logan? Can you prep for a full resus and a needle aspiration?"

She puts a hand on Sloane's arm after slipping the phone back into her pocket. "I better get out there, but I'm glad you and Ethan are doing great. And who knows...?" She spins around when she reaches the door. "Maybe we'll even be pregnant together!"

"Yes," Sloane says to the empty room. "I think we will."

Chapter 9

E than leans toward his computer screen at his cubicle at Seattle Homicide, staring at a satellite photo of the waterfront mansion Sloane visited last night. He forces himself not to think about what she did in the hour she was there. He's still furious that she lied to him about it. Even so, he wishes he could take back his response to her in the kitchen, knowing he was only pushing her farther away.

But he can't understand how she could be so aloof. He felt so sick after sleeping with Rachel—even after he told her it would never happen again—that he knew he had to come clean. He had never been so scared in his life. Until now.

He opens a new window and searches the King County Assessor website for the address. The fifteen-thousand-square-foot home was purchased for twenty-six million dollars four months ago by Pacific Estate Management, LLC. Ethan leaves the assessor website and runs an Internet search for the company. His heart drops in his chest when he reads the headline at the top of the search.

BRODY CARR'S MYSTERIOUS NEW COMPANY: PACIFIC ESTATE MANAGEMENT, LLC

Sloane's words on the phone replay in his mind. *Thanks, Brody. I'll let you know how it goes.* Ethan skims the first sentence beneath the headline. *Pacific Estate Management oversees many of Brody and Chelsea Carr's personal matters, including the power couple's real estate holdings.*

Their names sound familiar, and he drums his fingers against his desk before typing *Brody Carr* into his Internet search bar. A headshot of a guy around Ethan's age tops the search. Beside the photo, in bold letters: *Brody Carr, entrepreneur and founder of The One.* His net worth is listed as 1.4 billion dollars.

Ethan has never used the dating app, which had been around for over a decade, but everyone knew what it was. He recalls Sloane mentioning once that the app's founder had been her chemistry lab partner in college. Beneath Brody's headshot are several photos of him and a stunning blonde. Ethan's eyes travel to his biography on the right side of the screen. Brody Carr married Australian model Chelsea Nesbitt in 2016.

He sits back in his chair. He wouldn't have thought it would matter *who* his wife was having an affair with. But learning he was a billionaire dating app founder somehow made it sting worse. *How could this be happening?* Ethan examines the photo of Brody, smiling with his arm around his wife.

Behind him, his partner's phone rings as Ethan runs a new search for Chelsea Carr. A headline from last week appears at the top.

EX-MODEL CHELSEA CARR STEPS OUT WITHOUT WEDDING RING AT NY FILM FESTIVAL, SPARKING SEPARATION RUMORS

"We're on our way," he hears Jonah say.

Ethan clicks on the article as Jonah slaps him on the shoulder.

"Hey, we're up. That was McKinnon. Patrol just called in a man found stabbed to death in his apartment in the U district. They already have his neighbor in custody. According to another apartment resident, she came out of the victim's apartment covered in blood screaming that she killed him." After standing, Jonah leans forward to see what Ethan is looking at. "Unless you need to stay here and catch up on celebrity gossip."

Ethan closes his laptop and turns to see Jonah grinning at his own joke. Despite the churning in his stomach, he cracks a smile as he pulls on his suit jacket. "That's all right. I think I've had enough for today."

Chapter 10

Her house is depressingly quiet when Sloane steps inside. Exhausted, she sets her purse on the quartz kitchen counter before pouring a glass of Chardonnay. She thinks about Evelyn, going home to her twin girls, who are probably already tucked in bed by Ming, waiting for their mother to kiss them good night. Sloane imagines Ming rubbing Evelyn's feet, listening to the details of her day, before pushing the image from her mind.

When she checked her phone at the end of her shift, she had a message from Ethan saying he got a new case and would probably be working all night. His text was short. Cold. No *I love you*, or *good night*, or *sorry for being an ass this morning*. Wine in hand, she heads upstairs.

She moves past the kitchen barstools she ordered last month from Restoration Hardware. When Ethan learned that all together they cost what he makes in a month, he suggested she return them, not seeming to realize that after what he did, he was in no position to ask.

She hasn't heard from Brody since last night, but she's not worried. The look on his face when she pulled out of his drive told her he wanted more. A man like Brody Carr wouldn't stop short of getting what he wanted. She has the next two days off, and she's sure that by the end of them, Brody will reach out to her again.

She slows when she comes to the framed photo of Ethan's graduation from UCLA. Ethan is flanked by his parents. Sloane grips the banister and studies their beaming smiles. For Sloane, her college and medical graduations served as a reminder of how utterly alone she was. She fingers the gold heart on her necklace her mom gave her for her eighteenth birthday, remembering the night only days later when her mother never came home from work.

She had no one waiting to congratulate her—or take a photo with—at her college and medical school graduations. No one to call for support during the stress of exams while she worked herself through medical school. She can hardly imagine what it was like for Ethan, having wealthy parents who regularly topped up his bank account without even being asked.

She looks away from the photo, thinking of the icy words she spurted at Ethan this morning. *Not all of us grew up with rich, doting parents who made everything easy for them.* Was her resentment over his upbringing partly to blame for their relationship problems?

She dismisses the thought as she continues up the stairs. *Maybe.* But it was a far cry from Ethan's betrayal. She wouldn't be so defensive about her own childhood if Ethan didn't expect her to apologize for being driven to succeed. He'd never understand what it's like to have nothing and to feel powerless about it.

She stops when she moves past the guest room. She turns on the light, staring at the unmade bed in the space she and Ethan planned to turn into a nursery. She takes a sip from her wine, remembering the first time they met. Ethan came to interview a shooting victim she had stabilized. She'd seen him in the ER before, but had never spoken to him. She caught several of the younger nurses making eyes at him when he flashed a grin past the nurses' desk, a dimple forming on one side of his cheek.

He strode through the emergency room with a confidence that bordered on cocky, but Sloane admired the kind way she'd seen him interact with victims and their families. It was easy to see that he was good at what he did, and that it mattered to him.

"Hi. Um...I'm Ethan."

She looked up from a patient's chart to see him leaning against the nurses' desk. The color of his suit matched his dark hair.

"Oh. From Seattle Homicide, right?"

"Yeah." His blue eyes seemed to be twinkling at her. "I was—"

"The gunshot—"

They spoke at the same time, and he smiled. "Sorry, go ahead."

"I was just going to say that your gunshot victim was just moved to the fourth floor."

He broke eye contact with her for a split second, looking at the desk before returning her gaze. "Actually," he cleared his throat, and she realized he was nervous. "I was wondering if you might want to grab a coffee with me sometime?"

Sloane's eyes widened. Ethan's face flushed, and Sloane caught a young, single nurse cast a glare in their direction as she moved past.

"Ethan!" his older, balding partner called from down the other side of the nurses' station. "You ready?"

Ethan kept his eyes on Sloane. "Or dinner?"

He grinned.

Sloane grinned back before she could catch herself. "You don't even know my name."

"I guess that will give us something to talk about." He glanced at her ID badge clipped to her scrubs. "Dr. Loewen. How about dessert?"

"Marks! Let's go." His partner rolled his eyes before turning down the hall.

Ethan pulled his card from his suit pocket and held it toward her. "He loves working with me."

Sloane stifled a laugh as she took the card.

"How about we do all three?" he said, moving away from the desk. "Coffee, dinner, then dessert."

"I'll think about it."

"Please do." A dimple appeared on his cheek when he smiled, before following his partner.

She remembers looking at his card after he left, thinking there was something different about him. That life might be more fun with him by her side. And for a while, it was.

Her phone vibrates in her scrub pocket, tearing her thoughts back to the present. It was probably the hospital, asking her to come in for an overtime shift tomorrow. But when she lifts it from her pocket, she sees it's not the hospital. It's Brody.

Sloane takes a deep breath. She presses *Accept* and lifts the phone to her ear. "Hi."

"Hey."

His husky voice reminds her of last night.

"I'm sorry for last night," he says. "I can't stop thinking about you. And I want you to know that things between my wife and I are over. For good. I'm waiting on my legal team before I make a public announcement."

"Brody, I—"

"Look, I know this might seem crazy, but I want to see you again. Whatever this is between you and me, I don't want to lose it. Come away with me for the weekend. We can leave tomorrow. I'll fly us—no one will know. I have a very secluded home on San Juan Island where we can be alone. If you want me to go away, I will. But I had to tell you how I feel."

A weekend in the San Juans getting showered with attention from the billionaire app founder would be a lot better than sitting around an empty house or picking up another understaffed hospital shift. And it would get Ethan's attention a lot more now that he had learned where she was last night. But there is a risk it could drive him away completely.

Sloane turns off the guest room light. *Let Ethan be the one to come home to an empty house and wonder where I am.*

"What time should I meet you?"

Chapter 11

B rody grins at Sloane from the seat beside her as the float plane's propellers rumble to life. There is hardly a cloud in the sky, and the October sun glistens against the deep blue of Lake Washington.

"Ready?" His voice comes through her headset.

"I think so."

He taxis away from his dock, past the boathouse and superyacht moored in the adjacent boat slip. Sloane tilts her head to admire the sleek white boat that had been too dark for her to see the other night from Brody's patio. The vessel towers a few stories above them and has to be over one hundred feet long.

Having gotten home in the middle of the night, Ethan was still asleep when Sloane had left that morning. She left him a note saying she went in for an overtime shift, knowing he would call the hospital that night when she didn't come home. She smiles thinking of him kicking into detective mode, wondering where she was.

Brody scans the surrounding waters as he taxis toward the middle of the lake. He turns south and glances out the windows again before pushing in the throttle. Sloane admires the stunning view of snow-covered Mount Rainier in the distance before looking out her side window as they cruise over the sapphire blue water, forming a wake behind them. Brody pushes in full throttle before pulling back on the yoke.

Sloane feels a wave of excitement as they lift off from the lake and climb over Mercer Island before Brody banks to the right. They didn't say much when Brody met her in his driveway, although the tension between them was undeniable. He hugged her when she got out of her car. The feel of his embrace, Sloane noticed, was starting to become familiar. They held each other for a long moment before he took her overnight bag, and they walked hand-in-hand through the pristine grounds to the dock.

Now, as they ascend over downtown Seattle, Sloane spots Bayside Hospital, and the Seattle Police Headquarters. Tears spring to her eyes.

"Beautiful day for a flight."

Feeling Brody's hand on her knee, she blinks back her tears and looks away from the buildings below.

"I'm really glad you said yes," he adds.

Brody continues to bank right until they soar over Elliott Bay. As they head north over Puget Sound, he straightens out. An airliner appears in the sky, breaking through a thin patch of clouds several thousand feet above them.

Sloane squeezes his hand. "Me too."

She gazes out the window beyond him at the ferry pulling into Bainbridge Island, where Ethan took her on their first date.

"Are you sure you don't want a bite?" Ethan held out his spoon topped with pineapple-flavored shaved ice.

Sloane smiled. "I'm sure."

Ethan hadn't been kidding about taking her for coffee, dinner, and dessert all in one date. After getting coffee in Pioneer Square, they walked onto the ferry to Bainbridge Island, where they had dinner at an old, charming pub overlooking a marina filled with sailboats and small yachts.

"So, why did you become a doctor?"

Cold water rushed over the top of Sloane's bare feet as Ethan plopped the spoonful of shaved ice into his mouth. When she had spotted Ethan walking into the coffee shop earlier that night, she felt a rush of nervous excitement. Having seen nearly every trauma under the sun, she couldn't remember the last time she felt a rush of nerves like that. There was a slight tremble to Ethan's hand when he handed her latte to her, and she knew he was nervous too.

They quickly engaged in an easy-flowing conversation, Ethan sharing about growing up in California with two high-power attorneys for parents, and Sloane about being raised in Seattle by a single mom. Soon, her nerves faded away.

The beach was quiet for a Saturday evening in July as they walked along the water's edge between the ferry dock and marina. Aside from a woman walking her dog, they were the only ones there.

"Crystal—my mom—died in a car accident right after I graduated from high school." Having felt too young to be a mother when Sloane was little, Crystal taught Sloane to call her by her first name. When Sloane got older, Crystal decided she was ready to be called Mom. But, by then, it felt too strange to call Crystal something different from the name Sloane had used the first thirteen years of her life. "Her car hit a telephone pole at over fifty miles per hour when she was coming home from a double shift at the restaurant where she worked." She'd never *forget being jolted awake in the middle of the night by the police officer's unrelenting raps on her front door. After a fight, Crystal had kicked out her boyfriend of seven years, leaving herself solely responsible for paying the rent on his suburban Seattle house. Sloane dipped her head, watching her feet sink into the sand. There were no skid marks, and she'd never know whether Crystal fell asleep at the wheel or ended her life on purpose. "When I got to the ER, they had revived her to the point of consciousness, and I was able to tell her I loved her before she went into a coma. But she died two days later." Sloane fingered the woven strap of her wedge-heeled sandals in her hand. "After experiencing what it's like to lose someone you love, I find purpose in being able to prevent that from happening to someone else. When I can." She also craves the control and the feeling of belonging in society she gets from being a physician when she never had any of those things growing up. But that's probably better kept to herself for now.*

"I'm sorry about your mom." Ethan grabbed her hand as a ferry pulled into the dock at the end of the beach.

It was the first time they touched, but there was something familiar about the feeling of her hand in his.

"Thanks. It's hard to believe she's been gone fifteen years." She turned, meeting his denim blue-eyed gaze. "On a lighter note," she said, changing the subject, "your homicide partner seems...nice." She bit her lower lip as a smile pulled at her mouth.

Ethan laughed, and a dimple formed on one side of his face as he stuck his spoon into what was left of his shaved ice. "Oh, you noticed his super bubbly personality?" He shook his head. "Oh, man. Did you know when I got up to the fourth floor that day to interview our shooting victim, he had locked himself in the elevator?"

Now it was her turn to laugh. "Wait, how does that even happen? Aren't there buttons you can push to get out?"

"He took a patient transport elevator, thinking it would be quicker. But he didn't realize you needed a hospital keycard to get to another floor. He pushed so many buttons at once in his impatience to get upstairs that it locked up. It took a hospital maintenance worker over a half hour to get him out. So, I ended up interviewing our victim alone.

"I hope I never get like that," he added when Sloane's laughter faded. "Bruce is just waiting to retire. Trying to squeeze the last of his full paychecks before he goes out on his pension. It's a job to him, nothing more."

Sloane thought of seeing Ethan talking with victims' families in the ER. He seemed to genuinely care for them.

A bald eagle dove into the water straight out from where they stood. After a splash it emerged with a small salmon wriggling between its talons.

"But it's not for you."

He shrugged. "It's what gets me up in the mornings. My mission." He took the last bite from his now melted shaved ice. "Homicide victims don't have a voice. It's my job to speak for them."

Sloane admired the square lines of his jaw as Ethan gazed at the city lights illuminating the darkening skyline across the Sound. It was the first time she'd met someone who seemed to match her ambition. And Ethan's wasn't selfish-driven; he was purpose-driven.

There was an intensity in his voice when he talked about his work. He was different. And she liked it.

Chapter 12

The flight to San Juan Island is shorter than Sloane expected. In less than an hour, Brody descends toward a calm channel between San Juan Island and a smaller island across the narrow waterway. Despite being in a float plane, there is something unsettling about plummeting to the emerald water's surface. She shoots a glance at Brody, who appears completely calm as he guides the plane toward the channel.

"I can't believe you've never been to the San Juans," he says.

Sloane grips the side of her seat as they rapidly descend to the water. "We didn't travel much growing up." By *much*, she means never.

According to Sloane's mother, Crystal was always too much for Sloane's strict grandparents to handle. Having been a surprise pregnancy when her mother was forty-four, Crystal was raised by parents a generation older than most of her friends. Crystal's parents never quite knew how to manage their daughter's wild side. Not to mention her striking beauty. When Crystal got pregnant straight out of high school, her parents kicked her out of the house.

Sloane's father went to prison for auto theft three years later, and Crystal packed up her Firebird with Sloane and their few possessions, leaving the small, eastern Washington town for Seattle and never looking back. Sloane's father died in prison a few years later, and Crystal went from being financially dependent on one deadbeat boyfriend after another. Sloane was lucky to get new clothes the few times her mother could afford to buy them.

In her periphery, Brody eases the yoke forward. A colony of harbor seals basks in the sun on a small rocky island that protrudes from the channel. A couple lift their heads as the plane approaches. Sloane closes her eyes seconds before they make impact with the water. The plane glides smoothly across the surface before slowing to a stop. When she opens her eyes, Brody is grinning at her.

"Did I worry you?"

She exhales. Then, feeling ridiculous, she lets out a short laugh as she releases her grip from the edge of her seat.

A splash catches her attention out her side window. She turns to see the seals jumping into the water. Brody taxis toward a long jetty beside a tall, rocky cliffside and moors the plane next to a boat less than half the size of his one on Lake Washington. After climbing out of the plane onto the jetty, Sloane reads the name on the side of the faded vessel: *Miss Saigon*.

Unlike the megayacht moored at Brody's Lake Washington dock, this boat with its faded paint job and rust-stained exterior shows wear from decades of use. Not what she expected to see at the billionaire's weekend island home.

"She was my dad's." Brody stops beside her with her overnight bag slung over his shoulder. "He passed a few years ago and left her to me." Brody moves up the jetty, and Sloane follows beside him. "I spent nearly every summer on that boat as a kid. My dad would plan a trip to the San Juans every year. He, my mom, and I would stay on the boat and travel around to different islands and scuba dive."

"You scuba dived as a kid?" Sloane tries to hide her surprise. Remembering the shy, nerdy guy he was in college, she pictured the app founder growing up behind a computer screen. Or video games.

"My parents were both divers, and they taught me to dive when I was eight."

"You are not at all what I expected."

"Should I take that as a compliment?"

She grins when he catches her eye. "I guess I just expected, as an app creator, that you grew up more...indoors."

He chuckles, and Sloane can't help laughing herself.

She admires the color of the water lapping against the dark cliffside. "The water is so much greener than the Sound."

She steps off the jetty and follows Brody up a steep wooden staircase, noting the ease with which he climbs the steps while carrying their bags. She wonders if Ethan has called the hospital yet and found out she was never scheduled for an overtime shift.

"I don't scuba dive much anymore. I started freediving after I left college," he says, turning back to Sloane. "And now that's all I want to do."

Sloane is out of breath when they near the top of the staircase. She pauses to take in the view behind her, gripping the railing tighter as she looks at the water below. She was too busy envisioning Ethan fuming over her lie to realize how high they climbed.

Brody turns and offers his hand after he reaches the top. "It's breathtaking, isn't it?"

Sloane tears her eyes from the staircase and takes his hand. Their faces are only inches apart once he helps her to the top landing. Her heart is pounding, and she's not sure if it's from her fear of heights or Brody's proximity to her.

"You can't get a much clearer day than this."

Sloane follows Brody's gaze over the water, settling on the islands across the channel. The view is breathtaking—she can see all the way to Canada—but all Sloane can think about is Ethan. She pictures him struggling to stay focused on his work tomorrow, knowing she's off somewhere having a wild fling with billionaire Brody Carr.

Brody grabs her hand and leads her up a stone pathway through the trees.

"I have a full-time caretaker who normally stays on the property. But he's not here this weekend, so it's just you and me."

Sloane stops when the three-story mansion's peaked rooflines come into view at the end of the path. It's a completely different architectural style to Brody's modern home on Lake Washington but looks to be even bigger.

"Wow."

Brody grins. He lets go of her hand to unlock the craftsman wood door at the rear of the house. She follows him inside, taking in the huge cobblestone fireplace, vaulted wood ceilings, and stone floors. No expense had been spared in giving the mansion a rustic, yet luxurious feel, including the chandelier made of antlers. Sloane gazes at the exposed knotty pine beams above them. Somehow, the home manages to feel cozy despite its enormity. They pass by a dining room with bay windows offering a stunning view of the surrounding San Juan Islands. It looks like something out of *Architectural Digest*.

"This is amazing," she says.

"Thanks, I'm glad you like it. It's one of my favorite places to be. This home was my first major purchase after I..."

Sloane smiles. "Got rich?"

"I was trying to think of a more tactful way to put it. But yeah." He laughs, leading her up a craftsman wood staircase. "I've always loved these islands. Growing up, I never dreamed I'd be able to afford a place like this one day. But the best part of being here isn't this house. It's being on the water. Or even better, being underneath it."

Sloane's pulse quickens as Brody slows in the upstairs hallway beside an open doorway. He motions for her to step inside. "After you."

Sloane steps toward the four-poster bed, staring out at the view beyond several large windows. She feels Brody behind her and spins around. His eyes search hers after he sets her bag on the bed, and she takes a step toward him. She presses her palms to his chest and lifts her mouth to his, but he steps back before their lips meet.

"Brody..."

He takes both of her hands in his and flashes her a playful smile. "There'll be time for that later. How about I take you on an adventure?"

Chapter 13

"Where are we going?" Sloane calls out to Brody over the rumbling engines of *Miss Saigon*.

He takes his hand off the wheel and points out the window. "See that island over there?"

Sloane looks across the channel at a small, tree-covered island with a stretch of gray sand beach in the middle.

"I own it."

The wind has picked up since they arrived, and the yacht dips after going over a low swell. Sloane presses her hands against the dash to steady herself.

She turns to Brody. "The whole island?"

He nods, pushing the throttle forward. She smiles to herself. *Of course, he does.* Sloane keeps her hands against the dash as they cruise toward the island, enjoying being on the water in what feels like the first time in forever. Looking at Brody behind the helm of the well-used cruiser in his faded baseball cap, he doesn't seem like a billionaire dating app founder. He catches her staring and grins. Sloane feels a warmth rise to her cheeks as he slows when they near the island.

Instead of continuing toward the dock at the end of the beach, Brody idles the engines before moving to the front of the boat to drop the anchor. Sloane spots a raccoon swaggering across the rocky hillside beside them.

"Aren't we going ashore?" Sloane asks when Brody returns.

He throws the boat into reverse before killing the engine. "We can. But I thought first we could have lunch on the boat. Sound okay?"

"Oh. Sure." Now that she thinks about it, it has been hours since she's eaten. But it's a feeling she's gotten used to after so many shifts in the ER.

Brody turns to the kitchenette behind them and opens the mini fridge. "I wasn't sure what you like to eat, so I had them prepare a little bit of everything."

Them...being his staff, Sloane thinks, taking a seat at the table.

Brody looks inside the fridge. "There's Caesar salad, chef salad, Dungeness crab, croissant sandwiches, a cheese platter, and fruit."

"A croissant sandwich and fruit sounds great."

Brody sets a fruit platter on the table, along with a couple of plates from a cupboard beside the fridge. He places a sandwich on each one.

"What do you want to drink? There's sparkling water. Iced tea. Wine. Beer."

"Wine would be great." *Why not?*

After effortlessly uncorking a bottle from the fridge, he pours two glasses before sitting beside her. His leg brushes hers. While Brody will never be Ethan, she feels a rush at the thought of being with someone different than the man she's been married to for the last ten years. A thrill of not knowing what's about to come next. She wonders with a sinking feeling if that's what Ethan felt before he slept with his homicide partner.

He lifts his glass to hers. "Cheers."

"Cheers." She takes a sip.

"We're sitting on top of the best dive spot in all the San Juans. I used to scuba dive in this area with my parents. So, when the island went up for auction a few years back, I had to have it. Now I freedive it."

Sloane grabs a bunch of grapes and sets them onto her plate, thinking about the freediving medal displayed at his Medina home. "How deep did you dive at those freediving competitions?"

"One hundred meters."

Sloane coughs, nearly choking on her grape. "That's over three hundred feet! How is that even possible?"

Brody smiles. "You train—your body, and more importantly, your mind. To hold your breath for several minutes, while staying calm, despite the increasing pressure and darkness."

"How?"

"Physically, by learning to control your diaphragm, and to increase your lung capacity through lung packing."

"Lung packing?"

He nods. "You gulp air into your already inflated lungs using a muscle contraction like swallowing. It forces more air into the...whatever those small air sacs are called."

"Alveoli. Seems like that could cause a pneumothorax."

"A what?"

"Air leaking out from the lungs causing them to collapse."

"Oh, right. There are risks, and that's why you train and refine your technique. But some divers have gone much deeper than me. The world record for free immersion freediving, which is what I did, is one hundred and thirty-two meters."

Sloane does a quick calculation in her head. That was over four hundred feet. It seems unfathomable.

"In free immersion, you have no propulsion equipment, and you can only pull on the rope to assist with the descent and ascent."

Sloane feels a shiver creep down her spine at the thought of plunging to the dark depths of the ocean, aching for oxygen while enduring the crushing pressure. "I can't see why anyone would risk their life like that. For what? Ego?"

Brody shakes his head. "Freediving isn't about that. You do it for the dive itself. Mentally, you learn to succumb to the depths. Finding peace in the absence of all stimuli. Using the lack of light and sound to go inside yourself. The freedom of being one with the water, at a depth few people have ever reached, mastering your fears and surrendering to the darkness by allowing yourself to be carried into the deep." He stares out the window at the water, as if forgetting she was there. "When you get to about forty meters, it feels like your natural buoyancy is reversing, and the ocean starts pulling you down. It's a freefall that feels like you're flying."

Except you're sinking, Sloane thinks.

"It's an inner stillness that is unlike any other human experience. The only time I've ever felt pure joy. You let go of everything, even the urge to breathe. Your heart rate slows. Some divers have recorded a heart rate of only ten beats per minute."

"That would induce unconsciousness." Sloane gapes at him, and Brody laughs.

He shakes his head. "But in freediving, it doesn't."

"Huh." Sloane sits back, intrigued by the physiology of it all.

Sloane studies him as the boat sways gently from the swell of the water. How can someone be so incredibly successful, while also being so relaxed? He appears lost in thought for a moment until he tears his eyes away from the water and stands from the table.

A mischievous look comes over his face as he clasps his hands together. "I have a surprise for you."

Chapter 14

"I guessed on the size," Brody says in one of the boat's two small cabins, as Sloane lifts the hooded wetsuit out of the shopping bag.

Beneath it is a white string bikini. Sloane recognizes the signature Gucci interlocking gold G on the sides of the bikini bottoms.

"I'm not sure I—"

"Don't worry. We won't go very deep. I have long fins to help us dive down and come back up quickly." He places his hand on the small of her back. "Once you see how beautiful it is down there, trust me, you won't want to come back up."

"You mean until I need to breathe?"

She turns and allows him to pull her toward him. He brings his mouth to hers and kisses her slowly before pulling away. His hands travel down her arms as he steps back, and she realizes she wants more.

"I'll meet you on the rear deck. You're going to love it."

She watches him go before closing the door behind him. She bites her lip and pulls the tiny bikini out of the bag, glad that she manages to squeeze in Pilates five days a week, despite her long hours. She glances at the closed cabin door before pulling off her shirt. Being on a boat like this, alone—and romantic—should be something she's doing with Ethan. Why had they never done anything like this? They hadn't taken a vacation in years.

She finds Brody sitting on the back of the boat with his feet in the water after she emerges from the cabin. She feels ridiculous in the hooded wetsuit as she steps onto the rear deck, but Brody's attention is fixed on the water.

She takes a seat beside him, spotting a bald eagle watching them from a tree on the island. "How come your wetsuit doesn't have a hood? I feel like an astronaut, and you look like a surfer."

She dips her feet into the cold water. "*Brrr!*"

"You look beautiful," he says. "Like you were made for this. Here." He hands her a pair of long fins and a dive mask.

She slips the fins on first, wondering if they belong to his wife. She pushes the thought aside and pulls the mask over her head.

"All good?"

"I think so."

He dons his mask. "It's only about fifteen feet here, and the flippers will make it easy to kick to the bottom. Ready to jump in?"

She stares at the bright green water lapping against the boat as she scoots to the edge. "No." She pushes herself off the side and inhales a sharp breath, despite the wet suit. "Oh, that's cold!"

Brody eases into the water beside her. "You'll get used to it. Once the water inside your wetsuit warms from your body heat, you'll feel fine."

She glides her legs through the water, allowing the flippers to keep her afloat.

"You good?" he asks.

She nods.

"All right." He points a finger toward the water. "Let's go."

She draws a deep breath and follows him beneath the surface. She's surprised at the visibility in the green tinted water as she dives beside Brody toward the sea floor. Velvety ribbons from bull kelp float beside them, like an underwater forest, as he takes her hand. The long strands of kelp extend all the way to the rocks at the bottom. She kicks her legs, allowing the fins to propel her toward the colorful ocean floor. White particles dance through the water, making it feel like they're swimming through a snowstorm.

It's nothing like the dull green and brown colors she expected. The sea life around them is a bright array of orange, red, pink, and purple, and seems like it should belong in the tropics. It looks just like the photograph on the wall of Brody's Medina mansion, which she realizes wasn't taken at a tropical reef, but here. Perhaps even in this very spot.

Her lungs are already aching when they near the bottom, and Brody points to a crab moving across a rock. She motions toward the surface, and Brody nods. Together, they kick to the top. Sloane sucks in a sharp breath as her face breaks through the water.

"What do you think?" Brody asks. "Do you want to go back to the boat?"

Sloane shakes her head. "Let's go again."

He grins. "Okay."

She sinks beneath the surface with her hand in Brody's, enjoying the warmth and strength of his grip as they glide through the cold water. She kicks harder this time to reach the bottom before she feels the burning urge to breathe. She takes in the colorful sea floor as they glide slowly over purple urchins and yellow sea sponges. Ignoring the increasing ache in her lungs, she points to an orange starfish.

There is something magical about being down here, so far removed from all her worries. It's like they're in another world, one with just the two of them. She feels something pull her backward and turns to Brody, who is focused on a jellyfish moving above them.

Sloane spins to see what is tugging at her and finds a large piece of bull kelp wrapped around her leg. She flips over to reach for the kelp, but instead manages to wrap it another time around her ankle. She swims for the surface, but the kelp immediately drags her down. Air escapes her mouth as she tries to call out for Brody.

She whips around, the bubbles from her mouth clouding her vision as she frantically claws at the kelp around her leg. She feels herself sink to the uneven sea floor. She flails her arms above her head in a futile attempt to ascend while the kelp keeps her tied to the bottom. Brody swims past her in a dark blur of movement as more air leaves her mouth.

Her lungs scream for oxygen when Brody cuts the kelp from her leg then wraps his arm around her waist and pulls her toward the surface. She kicks and thrashes her arms through the water in her panic for air. But Brody maintains his hold on her, putting a hand under her jaw until her eyes settle on his. He moves his hand from her face, touching his index finger to his thumb to give her the OK signal.

She stops fighting, allowing him to propel them toward the surface. Her heart feels like it's beating into her throat. The agonizing burn in her lungs spreads to her sinus cavity when she opens her mouth, sucking in water. Brody clasps his palm over her mouth seconds before they break the surface.

She sputters out saltwater when Brody's hand falls away.

"Sloane!"

She coughs between gulps for air as Brody places her on her back. His wide eyes are panic-stricken, until he sees her take a couple deep breaths.

"That's it. Just keep breathing. Nice and slow."

She gives him the OK signal, even though she feels like she might pass out, as he encircles his strong arms around her torso from behind. She leans her head back on his shoulder, savoring every breath, as he tows her to the boat.

He helps her up the ladder first, and she rips off her dive mask after she steps onto the deck. The boat dips when he climbs aboard behind her. She grips the deck railing and stares over the side into the green water. If it wasn't for Brody, she would never have come up. Feeling his hand on her back, she tears her eyes away.

"I'm so sorry, I should've warned you about the bull kelp." He pats the knife inside the holder around his leg. "It's why I always dive with a knife." His eyes search hers after he pulls off his mask. "Are you okay? I can take us back to the house."

She closes the gap between them and reaches her arms around the back of his neck. There's a red ring beneath his cheeks from where his mask sealed, and she guesses her face is the same. He leans forward and kisses her, gently at first, before pressing his mouth harder against hers. She runs her hand down the back of his head as he pulls her toward him. Together, they move backward into the cabin.

She backs against the kitchenette counter, and Brody pushes his hips into hers. Sloane unzips the back of his wetsuit, tugging the material away from his shoulders. Brody pulls his arms out of the suit, placing his palms on either side of Sloane's face. Biting her lip, she slides her hands down his bare chest and playfully pushes him toward the stairs leading to the bedrooms below. He goes down backward, taking her hand and pulling her against him when she reaches the bottom.

Their lips meet, and Sloane lets out a soft groan. She pulls away, breathing hard, as Brody unzips her wetsuit. Her heart beats hard against her chest as his hands run down the sides of her waist. With his hands on her hips, he guides her through the open doorway into the cabin at the end of the narrow corridor.

"Brody..." she whispers, as his lips travel down her neck in the dim light shining through the small porthole.

For the first time that day, any thoughts of Ethan are completely gone from her mind. They topple onto the bed and her body entwines with his.

"Sloane..."

Chapter 15

Crime-scene tape already blocks the driveway to the three-story Victorian when Ethan pulls in front of the home on Saturday night behind two patrol cars. The notorious home of Kurt Cobain sits just a few doors down on Lake Washington Boulevard. It's the first time Ethan's been called to a homicide in the water-view neighborhood. It looks like he beat the CSI van *and* his partner, since he was working downtown when the dispatcher called. Being the weekend, there was no one else in the homicide unit, but he didn't mind. Sometimes, he prefers to work alone.

An elderly couple stands at the end of the drive, taking in the scene. The woman's hand covers her mouth as the man puts his arm around her shoulders.

Ethan pulls out his phone before getting out of the car. Still nothing from Sloane. They hadn't spoken since their blowup in the kitchen yesterday morning. *What if she's really falling for this guy?* Even spending the day burying himself in his cases had barely taken his mind off it.

And where the hell is she? It was nearly two a.m. when Ethan got home last night, and when he woke, she was already gone. He called *and* texted her earlier after finding the note she'd left beside his coffee maker. When she didn't respond after a few hours, he had called the hospital, and they said she wasn't working today.

The time on his phone reads 6:45 p.m. *Call me. I need to know you're okay.* Although, what he really wants to know is what the hell she's doing with Brody Carr. He hits *Send* before climbing out of his car and strides toward the female officer standing beside one of the patrol cars.

There is just enough daylight left for Ethan to make out a bearded man sitting in the backseat. He's wearing glasses and stares at Ethan as he approaches the car.

"I'm Detective Marks from Seattle Homicide," Ethan says over the crackle of voices on the officer's radio.

The pin on her uniform reads *Officer Blair.*

"My partner and I were the first to arrive after the next-door neighbors called in a report of a shot fired. We have the husband in custody." She gestures toward the man in the car. "He was sitting at the kitchen table with a shotgun propped against it when we went inside. He didn't try to flee, just kept repeating that he shot his wife. We found her in the master bedroom with what looks like a close-range shotgun wound to the back of her head." She glances back at the house. "It's not pretty."

Ethan eyes the man inside the car, who begins to sob. "Did he say what happened?"

Officer Blair nods. "Says she was cheating on him. He said he caught her on the phone with her boyfriend before getting his shotgun from the garage and going back to their room and shooting her in the head."

Sloane's bathroom phone call with Brody is glued to the forefront of his mind when Ethan spots Jonah's Ford Fusion pull up to the curb.

The officer continues. "I ran this address, and there's no record of SPD responses or domestic violence history. But the neighbors said they've heard them screaming at each other before."

Ethan's phone pings as Jonah steps onto the sidewalk. Ethan checks the screen and sees Sloane has replied. *I'm fine.*

But he's only slightly relieved as he types a quick response. *Where are you?* He waits several seconds for her to respond, before sliding his phone into his suit jacket pocket.

She has to be with Brody Carr. What the hell were they doing together? Although part of him doesn't want to know.

Ethan assesses the husband in the back of the patrol car. The man's sobbing has ceased, and he leans his head against the window in silence.

He needs to talk to Sloane. Tell her he's sorry and make her forget about that guy. Before it's too late.

He forces the last thought from his mind and pulls a pair of latex gloves from his pocket as Jonah approaches.

"Thanks," Ethan says to the officer. "We'll go check out the crime scene inside and be back to take him downtown."

Chapter 16

S loane sips from her third glass of champagne as she reclines against Brody's chest, nestled between his legs in his oversized clawfoot tub. In the master bath, they're surrounded by windows on three sides, and the impending nightfall casts shadows on the evergreen forest just beyond them. The bathroom lights put them on full display to the outside, but they are only at risk of being seen by the deer feeding along the tree line.

Brody wraps his arm around Sloane's waist. "When I bought this place, I always imagined I'd bring my children here one day."

After making love on the boat—twice—they spent the afternoon cruising around several of the San Juan Islands. While she knew she'd have to sleep with Brody, she hadn't expected to enjoy it as much as she had. And for Brody to be so...likeable. Different than what she expected. Aside from her near drowning, it had been a perfect day.

Sloane feels his chest move beneath her head as he sighs.

"But Chelsea never wanted them. She hates kids."

Resting her thigh against Brody's, Sloane recounts the look of Evelyn's beaming face when she broke the news of her second pregnancy. "I do."

"You do?"

He sounds surprised. *He probably thinks if I'd wanted kids, I would've had them already.*

"I figured maybe you didn't—with your job and all. I'm sure you've seen a lot of terrible things. I can't imagine all the kinds of trauma you've worked on."

"I have." He was right. Her job had contributed to her not wanting children in the past. And not just from having witnessed the anguish of parents who'd lost a child, but the demands of the job itself. If she was going to do something, she wanted to do it right. Perfectly, actually. Having grown up with a less than perfect mother, Sloane had no desire to become one herself. It wasn't until recently that she felt secure enough in her work to be ready to balance the two. "But I still want to have a child."

It feels good to have Brody acknowledge the hard things she's seen. While Ethan deals with equally horrific events in his job, he's always assumed that she deals with it the same way he does—which is not wanting to talk about it.

Ethan's resentful words to her in the kitchen yesterday morning run through her mind. *All you've cared about is your career.*

When they returned to Brody's island mansion, Sloane had several missed calls and texts from Ethan demanding to know where she was. She hadn't expected him to get so riled up until later that night when she failed to come home. *All the better.*

She swallows back the rest of her champagne as Brody encircles his other arm around her chest. She smiles, relishing the feeling of being in his strong arms. She anticipated feeling satisfaction knowing Ethan is tormented by her affair. Not to feel understood, heard, and wanted. By Brody.

"Can I tell you a secret?"

He nibbles her earlobe. "Tell me all your secrets."

She bites her lip. "After Ethan cheated, I would sometimes fantasize about him getting killed in the line of duty. I've even prayed for it."

Brody's lips move away from her ear.

She waits for him to respond, but he remains deathly quiet. "I shouldn't have said that. I know it sounds horrible. Maybe it's the champagne. It's just that...sometimes it seems like I'd be happier without him."

Brody doesn't speak, and Sloane feels her pulse quicken.

His bare chest rises beneath Sloane's back as he sighs. "I can understand that. When I met Chelsea, she was athletic, driven, and fun. We used to freedive together when we were dating. But having so much money changed her, especially after we were married. She got mixed up in the wrong crowd, which is easy to do in LA. She didn't seem to get that people were just using her for what we had. I hoped moving up here would take her away from all that. But she's just as much into that lifestyle as ever. And hates me for moving us out of California."

Sloane relaxes against him.

"I often think if Chelsea and I had put our profiles into The One, we would've never been a match. It could've saved me all this heartache."

"Do you think we would?"

His lips return to her ear. "I know we would.

"You feel cold," he says. "You want to get out?"

"Yeah." She climbs out of the tub and reaches for a towel.

"Damn you're beautiful."

She catches him gazing at her from the tub. She can hardly remember the last time Ethan looked at her like that.

⁓

From Brody's four-poster bed, Sloane watches the lit-up ferry cruising between them and Brody's private island across the channel. "It's so peaceful here."

"*Mm-hm.*" Behind her, Brody kisses the top of her shoulder. "I should warn you that, knowing Chelsea, my divorce could be a drudging. A long legal battle. And a very public one at that. There's no prenup, and Chelsea's going to try and take every dime she can. It wouldn't even surprise me if she tries to publicly drag my name through the mud, just to spite me." Brody traces the side of her body with his hand. "But I don't want it to stop us from being together. I've already lived too long without you," he adds. "You know I liked you in college, right?"

"You *did?*" She feigns surprise.

"I was completely taken by you the first time I saw you walk into class wearing those low-rise jeans and that pink sweater."

She turns around. "You remember what I was wearing?"

"I'll never forget it. But after I left school, I was always too scared to talk to you. Until you ran into me at the Kirkland Market."

She runs her palm across his chest. "You mean when *you* ran into me?"

"Maybe it was fate that made us run into each other." He props himself up on his elbow and slides his hand down the groove beside her hipbone. "I'm falling in love with you, Sloane."

She came here this weekend so Ethan would *see* her. Not as a woman he's wronged. But as a woman he can't live without.

So why does she feel like she's falling in love with him too?

Chapter 17

Sloane is surprised to see Ethan's car in the garage when she gets home early Sunday evening. She expected him to be working all weekend. A waft of satisfaction comes over her when she lifts her bag out of the trunk of her Porsche. Was he so tortured about her fling with Brody that he stayed home, waiting for her to come through the door?

She never replied to Ethan's text asking where she was. Or the one he sent hours later demanding to know who she was with. He called several times since last night, but she ignored them all.

She's still reeling from her whirlwind escapade with Brody when she walks through the mudroom. Hearing football playing on the living room TV, she steels herself to face her husband of ten years. She sets her purse on the kitchen table when Ethan comes into the room. He eyes her overnight bag as she sets it on the floor.

"You want to tell me where you were this weekend?" He crosses his arms.

Despite enjoying her weekend with Brody, she's certain that nothing will ever compare to what she has with the man standing in front her.

His ocean blue eyes bore into hers. *Good*, she thinks. Let him worry about it. Let him *care*.

It's Ethan she wants. He's the reason she did this.

She refrains from smiling. "I went to the San Juans. I'd never been. And I needed to get away for a couple of days. Clear my head."

His face hardens.

"It was just what I needed."

"Who were you with?" His left eye twitches.

She clears her throat. He stares at her in cold silence, waiting for her response.

"I went alone."

He flexes his jaw before pulling a beer from the fridge. He pops the cap but doesn't take a drink.

"Then why'd you lie about being at the hospital?"

She shrugs. "I guess I felt guilty about taking a couple of days to myself when you've been working so hard that you never come home. Not even for our anniversary. Or my award gala."

He tries to keep his expression neutral, but the twitch of his eye tells her he's boiling inside. "Is that what this is? You're getting back at me?"

She smiles. "I just wanted to have a nice weekend. And didn't want to sit around the house all by myself."

"So, you went to the San Juans *all by yourself*?"

"Yep."

He sets his jaw in the way he always does when he's pissed.

As he should be.

Ethan sets his beer on the counter and steps toward her. "Didn't you tell me once you went to college with Brody Carr?"

She feigns confusion. "The guy from The One?"

Ethan narrows his eyes.

"Touchdown!" an announcer exclaims through the living room TV. His voice is quickly drowned out by the roar of the crowd.

"We were in the same class together before he dropped out. I didn't know him. Why?"

"You said you were chemistry lab partners." Ethan frowns. "Are you sure there's nothing you want to share?"

Her mouth feels dry.

She studies the look on his face. Ethan isn't going to let this go tonight. He's going to push until she confesses. It suddenly occurs to her this could be the end of them.

It was a risk, her fling with Brody. It could be the final straw that pushes them over the edge of no return. Ethan could tell her it's over.

"I'm sure."

He comes another step closer. She braces herself for what could be coming next.

She relaxes her shoulders, knowing if she hadn't done it, their marriage was doomed. It was all or nothing.

If this was the end, Brody would undoubtedly be happy to step in and take Ethan's place. But as she looks at Ethan, the two-day stubble on his face reminding her of when they first met, she knows no one will ever make her feel like he does.

He stops when their faces are only inches apart. "You know what I think?" He cocks his head to the side. "I think I'll go *take a couple days*, too. This house suddenly feels too small for the two of us." His shoulder bumps against hers when he brushes past her.

Sloane lets out the breath she was holding when she hears Ethan storm upstairs. She sits at the kitchen table. Ten minutes later, Ethan returns with his gym bag slung over his shoulder.

"You sure there's nothing you want to tell me?"

His voice is calm. But Sloane can tell by his flushed face that he's fighting to control the rage boiling inside him.

"I'm sure."

His expression goes cold. "Unbelievable," he huffs, as he turns for the door.

Seconds later, the door to the garage slams, rattling the kitchen cabinets behind her.

She reaches for Ethan's untouched beer and takes a swig as she hears his car peel out of their drive. The football game goes to commercial when she steps into the living room. Beer in hand, she sinks onto her couch.

That could have gone a lot worse. He didn't say he was leaving her for good. Even though he looked angry enough to. She'll give him a few days. Long enough for him to feel the burn of being betrayed.

But no more. Any longer, and there would be no coming back.

Chapter 18

L ying atop the king bed that feels much too big for one person, Ethan flips through the channels on the large flatscreen in his downtown hotel room, unable to concentrate on anything other than his cheating, lying wife. She must know that he knows. She can't really think he's that stupid, *can she*? Was she so swept away by Brody Carr that she forgot what he does for a living?

After leaving the house, he nearly went to a budget motel by the airport but thought better of it. If Sloane can take a weekend getaway to the San Juans with that billionaire asshole, he can spend a couple of nights in a five-star hotel. Especially when it was her lies that drove him out of the house.

While he drove, he ran an Internet search on his phone for Brody Carr and the San Juans and learned the app founder owns a home on San Juan Island.

He sets down the remote after letting the TV settle on a classic movie channel playing *Bullitt*. He checks his phone and feels a burst of fresh anger that Sloane hasn't even tried to contact him after he stormed out of the house. He tosses his phone onto the white duvet, chiding himself for being so desperate. *She* should be the one who's scared. Checking her phone, terrified of why he wouldn't pick up.

When he slept with Rachel, he immediately knew it was a mistake. He was *sorry*. But when he confronted Sloane tonight, she didn't even blink.

What happened to us? He knew on their first date that no other woman would ever come close to making him feel the way Sloane does. He never imagined they'd end up like this.

∾

Sloane tucked a strand of dark hair behind her ear that had blown across her face from the breeze as she leaned against the railing on the upper deck of the Bainbridge-Seattle ferry. Ethan admired the way her black sundress highlighted her slight curves perfectly, even in the waning daylight. He followed her gaze over the side at the calm, dark waters.

"What do your parents think of you being a detective? They must be so proud."

She was looking at him when he turned toward her. He chuckled.

"No." He shook his head. "My dad was livid when I told him I had applied to become a cop after he put me through law school. He said he was upset he wasted all that money, but that wasn't it. As a criminal defense attorney, he despised cops. I think he'd rather I had flunked out of high school than gone into law enforcement."

Sloane gazed at the few cars parked on the deck below. The ferry was nearly empty heading back to Seattle at this time of night.

"I don't think my mom is pleased either, but she's kind enough to at least keep it to herself."

"That must be tough."

Ethan suddenly felt guilty for complaining. At least he had parents.

"You managed to get through college and *med school without having parents to support you. That couldn't have been easy."*

She shrugged. *"I didn't know any different."*

Ethan admired her profile in the twilight.

"I just kept focused on my end goal. I got my pre-med degree in three years while working a couple of after-hours jobs. The fact that it was hard actually kept me motivated." She turned to face him. "The sooner I got through it, the sooner I could be a doctor, and start being the person I wanted to be.

"Wow. I must sound pretty pathetic to complain about my parents. You're incredible, you know that?" He looked into her dark eyes. "Being around you is inspiring. You make me want to be better."

Her long hair lifted in the wind behind her head as the ferry approached the Seattle waterfront pier. She smiled before gazing toward the city skyline beyond the water.

"It gives you a different perspective being out here. I'm in this city every day, but I never get to view it like this. To take a step back and actually enjoy it."

His eyes were on her when she tilted her face toward him. The city was beautiful from the water, its lights brightening with the setting sun. But for Ethan, it was nothing compared to what it felt like to be standing next to Sloane. Enjoying it with her. *"What city?"*

She laughed. *"Ethan Marks, do these lines really work for you?"*

"I'm serious." He'd never met anyone so beautiful and so smart. "Do you even have any flaws, doctor? There is something almost...superhuman about you."

She giggled before feigning a pensive expression. *"Hmm. Superhuman. Yes, I get that all the time."*

"I'm serious." He moved closer to her.

She grinned playfully. "So am I, detective."

"I was drawn to you the first time I saw you. There's something different about you."

Sloane's gaze fell to his mouth before returning to his eyes. "I was drawn to you too, detective." Her smile was replaced with a look of longing.

Ethan lowered his mouth to hers as the ferry horn blared from above, cutting though the stillness of the calm night.

∞

Ethan glances at his phone atop the down comforter. *What is she doing?* He wishes he would have taken the time to install the doorbell video app on their front porch that Sloane bought several months ago. If Sloane invites that dating app founder to *their* home, she's got another thing coming.

A tear slides down his cheek as he nurses the beer he grabbed from the mini bar and tries to focus on Steve McQueen racing the streets of San Francisco in his famous Mustang GT. But as much as he tries not to care, to hate Sloane for what she's done, he can't.

But there was no disappointment in her eyes tonight. There was something else. Something he didn't recognize. He's not sure whether he's more terrified to lose her or infuriated. The woman who came home and lied to his face is someone he doesn't know.

He checks his phone another time before he throws it across the room. It lands with a thud on the pull-out couch.

Bullitt goes to commercial. An attractive woman sitting on a park bench wearing a pencil skirt and white blouse fills the screen, her short dark curls reminding him of Sloane.

"Tired of dating one wrong person after another? Try The One. Where real connections are made to form lasting love. Join today and—"

Ethan flicks off the TV, his heart rapping against his ribs. He turns off the light beside his bed and puts a down pillow over his head after lying down, despite being way too amped to go to sleep. He closes his eyes, willing sleep to come while trying unsuccessfully to think of anything besides Sloane in the arms of Brody Carr.

It's going to be a long night.

Chapter 19

E velyn stands from her computer when Sloane marches toward the nurses' desk in the middle of the ER. Sloane just finished stabilizing a homeless man who'd been brought in with multiple stab wounds to the abdomen before he was taken to the OR. She pulls her personal phone from her scrub pocket—something she never carried on shifts before her fling with Brody.

She hasn't heard from Ethan since he stormed out of the house two nights ago. But she's not worried. If he was going to leave her for good, he would've done it already. She'll let her affair with billionaire Brody Carr sink in for one more night before she tells Ethan the truth.

"What's the ETA on the ambulance?" Logan asks from the doorway of one of the treatment rooms.

"They said they'll be here in five minutes." Evelyn sounds tired.

Sloane's stomach growls as she leans against the desk and sees she has a message from Brody. It was sent two hours ago. *When can I see you again?* She bites her lip and slides her phone into her pocket. She has to break it off with him. Now that their affair has served its purpose.

She thinks of the kiss she shared with Brody on his boat after he pulled her to the surface when she nearly drowned. It was the excitement of the affair, and the new-found attraction that she had been drawn to. Not Brody Carr. While it was fun, it would never compare to the deep connection she shared with Ethan.

"You better take a break while you can, Dr. Marks. It's shaping up to be one of those days," Logan says, before disappearing into the room behind him.

Evelyn yawns as she steps out from behind the nurses' desk.

"You look pale," Sloane says.

Evelyn shrugs, adjusting the stethoscope hanging around her neck. "I didn't sleep well. Threw up three times in the night."

The dark circles under Evelyn's eyes are the color of the Sound.

"Why don't you take a break?"

She shakes her head. "I've got a drowning victim coming in via ambulance."

"I'll take it. Go ahead."

"Are you sure? You've been here longer than me. You should go."

"It's fine," Sloane says, ignoring a stab of a hunger pang.

"All right. The patient coming in is a thirty-two-year-old female found unresponsive while diving near Alki Beach."

"Diving?"

Evelyn nods. "That's what the medic said. Actually, he called it freediving. She still had a weak pulse after her husband dragged her to shore but lost it shortly after the medics arrived."

The room suddenly feels cold.

"She's intubated," Evelyn adds. "And they're running a full code. At least the water is cold; it should give her a chance. Anyway, thank you, I could really use a Sprite."

"Hey, Logan," Evelyn says as she moves past the treatment room. "Sloane is taking the new one for me. I'm going on break."

"Okay." He heads toward the ambulance entrance. "You coming, Dr. Marks?"

She follows him without a word. When she reaches the sliding doors, she hears the ambulance in the distance.

Logan turns. "So, Evelyn told you what happened to the patient coming in?"

"She said she was...freediving?"

He nods. "Evelyn said she got caught in some kelp, apparently. By the time her husband untangled her, she'd been underwater for several minutes."

A knot forms in Sloane's stomach as she pictures Brody pulling his wife's limp body ashore. *It can't be.*

"And get this. When I checked to see if the patient's been admitted to our system, I saw her name is Chelsea Carr."

Sloane fights the urge to vomit as Logan steps toward her.

"Oh, yeah." Logan waves a hand through the air. "I forgot you don't keep up with celebrity news. Chelsea Carr's a model who married that guy who created The One," he continues. "I saw online they recently moved to Seattle. You think it's her?"

The sirens grow louder. Sloane stares at the lights pulling into the parking lot beyond the glass doors. Sloane feels numb. *This cannot be happening.*

Logan shrugs when Sloane doesn't respond. "I know, probably not."

The ambulance pulls to a stop, and Logan presses a button to open the doors. Sloane stands frozen in place as the medics pull the stretcher out of the back of the ambulance, relieved to see Brody Carr is nowhere in sight.

"We're taking her to treatment room six," Logan says as they wheel her inside.

One of the medics bags a breath through her endotracheal tube in between compressions. Two IV bags hang from a metal pole attached to the stretcher, pumping fluid into a vein in her arm.

"When we arrived and hooked her up to the cardiac monitor, she was in bradycardia with a heart rate of ten," one of the medics tells Sloane. "But by the time we got her intubated, it was gone. We started compressions and gave three rounds of code meds and a saline bolus on the way here."

He continues to recap their resuscitation efforts as Sloane compares the lifeless woman before her to the image on the wall of Brody's bedroom. She follows alongside as the medics maneuver the stretcher swiftly through the hallway, unable to tear her eyes from Chelsea's long blonde hair and mottled, pale-gray skin. She recalls the photo of Brody and his wife that resulted from her Internet search of the app founder months ago. There is no doubt in her mind that this woman is Brody's wife. She envisions what Chelsea must have felt during her final moments, remembering her own terror before Brody freed her from the kelp only days earlier.

"Dr. Marks?"

Sloane turns to see Logan looking at her expectantly when they reach the treatment room. The medics had already slid Chelsea off the stretcher and onto the hospital bed. She watches Chelsea's chest recoil with every compression.

"I said do you want me to give another round of epi?"

"Sorry." *Calm down.* "Um. Yes."

Logan pushes the syringe contents into Chelsea's IV. He looks at Sloane when the other nurse pauses compressions to allow the defibrillator to analyze Chelsea's heart rhythm.

"Maybe we should give Narcan," he says.

Sloane shakes her head. "It won't do anything."

"I just thought—"

"She drowned, *okay?*"

All eyes in the room turn toward Sloane, and she realizes she shouted the words. *Hold it together.*

She stares at the cardiac monitor displaying asystole. Logan sets down the defibrillator paddles at the absence of a heart rhythm and lifts his hands in the air. "Just figured it wouldn't hurt."

Sloane turns to one of the medics as Logan resumes compressions. She'll apologize to him later.

"What time did you initiate compressions?"

He checks his clipboard. "12:15."

Sloane glances at the clock on the wall. *Focus. You need to focus.* "Cease compressions."

The room is quiet as she assesses the cardiac monitor. A flatline appears. She puts her stethoscope to Chelsea's chest and listens for thirty seconds before removing her earpieces. "Time of death is 12:48 p.m."

Logan stops, shooting Sloane a wary expression when his eyes meet hers. He turns to an EMT, who is on his way out of the room.

"Where's her husband?" he asks. "The guy's a big deal."

The EMT nods his head. "I know. But he was really distraught, and we didn't want him to get in the way. A patrol officer offered to drive him here, so they'll probably be here any minute."

Sloane feels the floor sway beneath her feet.

"Excuse me." She pushes past the EMT out of the room, hearing Logan call her name when she steps into the hallway.

She covers her mouth with her hand as she hurries past the nurses' desk toward the breakroom. Evelyn looks up with a start when Sloane throws open the door. She rushes toward the water cooler and fills a cup with a trembling hand.

"Everything okay?" Evelyn asks.

"We lost her," Sloane says after guzzling her water. "I just need a minute."

"Sorry. I owe you one."

Sloane turns her face away. She puts her hands on her hips and stares at the floor, trying to slow her breathing. Her hospital phone rings inside her scrub pocket. She pulls it out, but sees she pulled out her personal phone instead.

Brody's text from earlier still appears on her home screen. *When can I see you again?* She closes her eyes and sees Brody wrapping the kelp around Chelsea's leg, pulling her down with his muscular arms to make it look like an accident. The same muscular arms that—

"Dr. Marks?"

She spins toward Logan's voice in the breakroom doorway.

"I just called you. Brody Carr is here and is asking about his wife."

Sloane exhales. "I'll be right there."

Logan steps inside the breakroom. "I only asked about the Narcan because Chelsea Carr went to rehab last year for an opiate addiction. It was in the news. I know it probably wouldn't have made a difference. I just thought—"

"We don't make medical decisions based off celebrity news. She drowned."

Evelyn raises her eyebrows at Sloane's sharp tone, as she lifts her Sprite to her mouth.

Logan nods, pressing his lips together. "I'll bring him back."

Evelyn takes a long drink from her Sprite as Logan disappears down the corridor, and Sloane tries to prepare herself to face Brody.

"You okay?" Evelyn asks, when Sloane moves toward the door.

"Yeah. Thanks, I'm fine."

After leaving the breakroom, Sloane spots Logan leading Brody toward his deceased wife's room. Her heart pounds against her chest. Brody's wearing a wet suit, looking exactly like he did before they made love for the first time on *Miss Saigon*. Except for the grief-stricken look on his face.

Logan gestures to her as she approaches. "This is Dr. Marks."

Brody's eyes meet hers, and she feels her heart catch in her throat. Brody stares at her blankly, giving no indication they've met before. Or that he texted Sloane hours ago, asking when he could see her again. "Is Chelsea..." Tears brim in his eyes.

Sloane swallows. "I'm afraid that despite our best resuscitation efforts, we were unable to revive your wife. Her pulse never returned after her heart stopped, when the emergency responders arrived."

Brody's chin quivers, and he hangs his head.

"She's right in here if you'd like to see her," Logan says.

Brody nods and follows him into the room. Sloane enters behind them, wishing she could run away. Chelsea's breathing tube is still in place, but a sheet has been pulled over her chest. She looks peaceful.

"Chelsea!" Brody kneels beside her, enveloping her limp hand inside his. He presses his forehead against the side of her face as his body heaves with sobs. "No, no, no!"

After a minute, Brody pulls away and sinks into a chair beside his wife's body. He buries his face in his hands. Sloane watches him in disbelief, disturbed by his convincing act as the grieving husband after what he did to his wife. If she didn't know better, she would have believed him herself.

"We're very sorry for your loss," Logan says. "Can I call you a chaplain?"

Sloane feels herself back out of the room. She can't breathe while standing in this tiny room beside her lover and his dead wife, watching him pretend her death was a tragic accident that's ripping him apart.

She collides with Evelyn when she bolts out of the room.

"Oh!" Evelyn shrieks.

"Sorry," Sloane mumbles and darts for the staff bathroom, feeling like the walls might cave in on her at any second.

"Sloane?" Evelyn calls out.

Once inside, she throws open the first stall in the row and locks the door behind her. She leans her head back against the side. *Just breathe.* She feels like she might throw up, even though she can't even remember the last time she ate.

She hears the bathroom door open as she leans her head over the toilet bowl.

"Sloane?"

It was Evelyn.

"Logan asked me to come see if you're okay."

Sloane presses her palms against the seat.

Evelyn moves toward the stall. "You're not pregnant, are you?"

Sloane thinks back to the weekend and takes a deep breath. She stands up. "No. It's just been a long day."

"I hear you. You sure you're all right?"

"I'm fine."

"Cool. Because there's been a double shooting in Pioneer Square. Both victims are en route. Matt and Anil are tied up with other patients, so I'll need your help."

"Great." Sloane flushes the toilet for good measure. "Be right there."

Chapter 20

S loane walks through the breakroom to get to her locker. Her shift from hell is finally over. She feels sick. Numb. *Brody's wife is dead, and it was no accident.* She's not sure how she managed to finish her shift without having a nervous breakdown, but somehow she did it.

Two of the dayshift nurses stand in the corner of the room with their eyes glued to the news playing on the large flatscreen TV. A dark-haired Seattle newscaster wearing a red blazer fills the screen. One of the nurses reaches for the remote and turns up the volume.

"Breaking news tonight as we learn that Australian-born model, philanthropist, and former competitive freediver, Chelsea Carr, has tragically died at the age of thirty-two."

Sloane stops and stares at the TV.

"Our sources tell us she was freediving off Jack Block Park near Alki Beach today with her husband, The One's founder Brody Carr, when she got tangled in bull kelp. By the time her husband managed to free her from the kelp and drag her to shore, she was unresponsive. She was pronounced dead shortly after her arrival at Bayside Hospital."

One of the nurses shakes her head. "So sad."

"Her recent rise to fame stemmed from her modeling career, but she will also be remembered for her work with the Children's Cancer Society. Ms. Carr broke the women's world record for free immersion freediving, diving to a depth of ninety-two meters on a single breath."

The news pans to an interview from 2012 with Chelsea wearing a wetsuit, a medal hanging from her neck. The same medal that was hanging on the wall at Brody's house. Sloane gasps, causing one of the nurses to glance at her. The freediving photo hanging on Brody's wall beneath the medal wasn't of him. It was Chelsea.

The reporter lifts a microphone toward Chelsea. "Can you tell us how it feels to dive over twenty stories deep on a single breath, knowing you're going deeper than any woman has before? How do you manage to stay calm during the dive?"

Chelsea leans toward the microphone. "When you reach about forty meters, you start to freefall. It feels like you're flying."

Except you're sinking.

"You let go of everything, even the urge to breathe. It's an inner stillness unlike any other experience. It's joy. Pure joy."

Chelsea smiles.

Sloane feels bile rise to the back of her throat. "Son of a bitch."

Both nurses turn and gape at her.

"What?" one of them asks, furrowing her brows. "Are you okay?"

Sloane keeps her eyes on the flatscreen.

"The dive is the easy part," Chelsea adds. "It's coming back up that is the challenge."

Sloane feels her chest tighten. She pushes past the nurses and throws the door open to the locker room. She needs to get out of this place.

Chapter 21

Sloane sinks against her leather seat after she pulls into her garage. Ethan's bay is empty. She goes inside, glad she doesn't have to face him. At least not yet.

She needs to be alone to process the day's events before she confesses her affair to Ethan. She sets her purse on the kitchen table and takes a glass from a cupboard. She turns on the faucet. But instead of filling her glass, she stares at the water, seeing Chelsea's cyanotic, lifeless body recoiling from Logan's chest compressions.

What really happened beneath the waters of Puget Sound that afternoon? Did Brody drown his wife? Or did she really get tangled in the kelp, and this time Brody looked on, watching her struggle to break free?

Sloane ran a quick search on her phone before leaving the hospital. She couldn't find any evidence that Brody ever freedived competitively. Only Chelsea. He lied and she fell for it.

But she lied too—about fantasizing that Ethan would get killed in the line of duty. She wasn't even sure why she'd gone that far, but when she said it, she needed him to think that *he* was the one for her. But now Chelsea is dead.

Goosebumps form on her arms as she moves her glass beneath the stream.

"Hey."

She jumps, spilling water across the floor when she whips around.

"Oh!" She brings a hand to her chest. "Ethan." She reaches behind her to turn off the faucet. "I didn't hear you come in."

"You left the garage door open."

Sloane searches his eyes, but his expression is unreadable.

"I did?"

He nods.

"Oh. It was a long day at work." She lifts her glass to her lips, hoping he doesn't notice the tremble of her hand.

Ethan must have heard the news about Chelsea Carr. It was everywhere. *You have to tell him. Before he thinks you had something to do with her death.*

She hadn't expected him to come home tonight. She hoped she would have more time to gather herself before she confessed the affair.

"I saw Brody Carr's wife died today." Ethan stops on the other side of the kitchen island. "In a freediving accident."

Sloane coughs. She sets her glass on the counter.

Ethan crosses his arms, his eyes intent on hers. "And she died at Bayside Hospital."

"Ethan." She presses her palms against the cold countertop. "There's something I need to tell you."

He watches her in silence as she moves around the island, stopping within arm's length of him.

This is not how this was supposed to go. "I've been having an affair with Brody Carr."

"I know."

"I *wanted* you to know."

His eyes roll to the side in disbelief, and he lets out a snort.

"Why? To get even with me?"

"More than that, Ethan. I want you to stop seeing me as the woman you've wronged. I need to be the one you can't live without."

He uncrosses his arms, pulling out of her reach. She examines his blue eyes for a sign he still loves her, but all she sees is suspicion.

"It's over. And it meant nothing. It was over as soon as I got back from the San Juans."

"Then why is his wife *dead?*"

He shouts the last word. Sloane flinches. "I...I don't know. It looked like an accident." As she says the words, she envisions Brody calmly swimming to the surface, towing his dead wife, thinking that his troubles were over. But she can't tell Ethan how she knows this. If he thinks Brody killed Chelsea, he might suspect her, too. "When she was brought in, I did everything—"

"Wait. *You* were the one who treated her?"

"Well, yes, but I didn't know it was going to be Brody's wife! I was just doing my job!"

Ethan's eyes seem to double in size. He steps toward her.

"There's going to be an autopsy. You know that, right? It will be up to the medical examiner to determine Chelsea's manner of death. If it's undetermined, there will be an investigation. And if your affair is brought to light, you could be implicated. Hell, Sloane, it could look like you finished her off when she got to the hospital!"

"Ethan!"

He turns and puts his hands on his head. "Why did it have to be *Brody Carr?* You couldn't have picked...*anyone* else?" he yells.

"It was an accident."

Ethan spins around. "You better hope it *was* an accident. And that there's no investigation."

"Wait!" Sloane follows after him when he marches out of the kitchen, relieved to see he's headed for the stairs and not the garage.

He stops when he reaches the base of the stairwell.

She reaches for his arm. "It wasn't supposed to go like this. If Chelsea's death *wasn't* an accident, I had no part in it. I would never do that. I did everything I could to save her!"

"After all your lies, how am I supposed to believe you?" He pulls out of her reach and starts up the stairs.

"Because you *know* me."

He turns when he gets to the top. "Do I?"

Chapter 22

"I need to see you two in my office."

Ethan's sergeant, Wade McKinnon, is standing beside his desk when Ethan looks up. He scoots back his chair and realizes he'd been staring at his computer screen long enough for the screen saver to appear. He stifles a yawn as he and Jonah follow McKinnon into his office.

Ethan hardly slept last night in the few hours he'd been home. The news of Chelsea's death—and learning Sloane pronounced her dead—rattled him. He recalls the look on Sloane's face when she confessed the affair and said it was over. Had she really done it only to get back at him?

He considers what Sloane said about wanting him to see her not as the woman he'd wronged, but as one he couldn't live without. What exactly did she mean?

Or had she come clean only because she knew he had already figured it out and was scared of what he might think after learning Brody's wife died? Either way it stung, and he isn't sure how he can ever trust her again.

He *is* sure that a man like Brody Carr would have a lot to lose in a divorce. But if his wife's death wasn't an accident, does that mean Sloane played a role?

"Have a seat." McKinnon moves behind his desk.

After closing the door to the bustling homicide unit, Ethan sits beside Jonah in the small windowless office. His mind replays Sloane admitting her relationship with the app founder as McKinnon leans forward. The sergeant folds his hands atop his desk.

"I'm sure you've heard the news that Chelsea Carr, wife of The One's founder Brody Carr, died yesterday."

Jonah nods. Ethan feels the blood drain from his face.

"Chelsea's parents have contacted the department. They're accusing her husband of killing her."

Ethan's eye twitches.

"According to them," McKinnon continues, "Chelsea had met with divorce attorney Adrienne Lamar and was planning to file for divorce this week. Apparently, Chelsea had incriminating photos of Brody Carr with that financier Mason Hachette and underage girls. They suspect he killed her to save himself the scandal, money, and possible prison sentence if Chelsea came forward with the photographs.

"Her parents are on a flight here from Sydney, Australia right now. They believe she had the photos on her phone. The ME has ruled Chelsea's cause of death as drowning, although we're still waiting on the official autopsy report. He's left the manner of death undetermined for now, pending our investigation. We are officially treating her death as suspicious, and I've assigned you two to the case."

Ethan shifts uncomfortably in his seat.

Jonah shoots him a look of excitement before turning to McKinnon. "Were there any witnesses to the drowning?"

McKinnon shakes his head. "They were diving off the shore of Jack Block Park, if you know where that is. South of Salty's at Alki Beach. So, it butts up against the shipping yard. According to the report from patrol, there was no one else on the beach. Not surprising for a dreary weekday in October. There's hardly anyone at that park, even in the summer."

Jonah raises his eyebrows. "I know that park. An old girlfriend of mine lived in West Seattle. She loved the view of downtown from that beach. There was never anyone there. Maybe that's why Carr picked it. So...it was Brody Carr that made the 911 call?"

McKinnon nods. "That's right."

Jonah stands from his seat. "Looks like we've got work to do."

Ethan can't bring himself to move.

"One more thing," McKinnon says. "There's already a ton of media attention surrounding her death. They're going to go nuts when they learn we're investigating her dating-app-founder husband for her murder. For now, we're giving the media as few details as possible. We don't want a media circus to hinder our investigation. And we need to get our hands on Chelsea's phone to see if we can find those photos."

"Got it." Jonah opens the door.

"You okay, Marks?"

Ethan realizes Jonah has gone back to his desk. He's alone with McKinnon, who is eyeing him strangely.

"Yeah." He forces himself to stand and follow his partner back to their cubicle.

Jonah turns to him when Ethan reaches his desk. "I'll draft the affidavit for the warrant for Chelsea Carr's phone." He slaps Ethan on the arm. If Jonah notices his partner's shock, he doesn't show it.

"You want to track down Brody Carr?" His lips lift into a wry smile. "Let's see what he has to say."

∞

Ethan and Jonah watch a yellow Ferrari speed into Brody Carr's circle drive from the front seats of Jonah's Fusion. After buzzing the intercom, they'd been let through the gated entrance to Carr's waterfront Medina home. When they approached the front door, Ethan braced himself for coming face-to-face with the man who had been sleeping with his wife. But Carr's housekeeper answered the door instead. She left them on the porch while she checked if her employer would see them. Moments later, she told them Carr's attorney was on his way, and he would speak to them once the attorney arrived. There was no offer to come inside, so they returned to Jonah's car while they waited.

"Subtle car," Jonah says as a tall man with slicked-back hair steps out of the Ferrari.

The attorney smooths his suit before striding toward the house. Ethan folds a stick of gum into his mouth before climbing out of the car. The same housekeeper opens the door after Carr's attorney rings the bell. This time, she holds the door open for Ethan and Jonah to follow.

Ethan eyes the security camera above the front entry before going inside, thinking of Sloane's visit after her award gala.

The detectives move behind the attorney through the mansion's main level, following in a trail of his strong cologne. While Jonah appears to take in the home's opulent surroundings, Ethan's thoughts are consumed with Sloane, envisioning her in this house—with Carr. An image of Sloane laughing in Carr's arms before they stripped off each other's clothes inundates his mind when Ethan enters a formal dining room with views of Lake Washington.

Carr stands from the table and shakes hands with his attorney. Ethan stares at the app founder. He's dressed in a button-down shirt with his brown wavy hair neatly combed back. Despite his wife dying yesterday, the billionaire's eyes look fresh—more well-rested than Ethan's.

Jonah extends his hand. "I'm Detective Nolan from Seattle Homicide."

Carr accepts his handshake. "Brody Carr."

He swings his hand toward Ethan. Ethan clears his throat and encloses his grip around the billionaire app founder's, wanting to throw a punch at his jaw. "And I'm Detective Marks."

Carr sits beside his attorney at the twelve-seat dining table. If he's aware of Ethan being Sloane's husband, his face shows no recognition of it. Ethan and Jonah sit opposite.

Carr is bigger than he looked in his online photos. His muscular chest and arms protrude beneath his fitted shirt. Ethan pictures them wrapped around Sloane before forcing the image from his mind.

"We're very sorry for your loss," Jonah starts.

Ethan eyes Carr's broad shoulders. It would have been easy for him to overpower his wife beneath the water, no matter how strong a swimmer she was.

Carr nods. "Thank you."

Beyond the bay windows at the end of the table, Ethan spots a float plane beside a huge yacht on Brody's dock. *Was it Carr's money Sloane was drawn too?* But he knows that's not it. Sloane is the most fiercely independent person he's ever known and despises how her mother was always financially dependent on men. Ethan returns his attention to Carr across the table. Knowing Sloane wasn't wooed by his wealth only makes him feel worse. It means there was something deeper between them.

"We're here because we're opening an investigation into your wife's death," Jonah says.

Carr glances at his attorney. "Why is that?"

"How was your relationship with your wife? You were separated, correct?"

Carr waits for his lawyer to give him a nod of approval. "Yes, we've been separated for two months. But we were working things out."

By sleeping with my wife. Ethan feels the urge to flip the table over and take Carr's neck in his grip at the same time. He resists them both. Instead, he locks eyes with The One's founder.

"Can you explain to us what happened yesterday while you and your wife were diving? How she died?" Jonah asks.

Before leaving the homicide unit, McKinnon replayed Carr's 911 call to the emergency operator for Ethan and Jonah. Carr had sounded every bit the distraught husband trying to save his dying wife.

"We used to freedive together a lot when we lived in California. It's something we both loved. So, we thought it might be a good way to try and rekindle things between us. Anyway, we went into the water together. The visibility wasn't great. We came upon some short pilings and a school of fish. I spotted a huge ling cod and swam after it. I thought Chelsea was coming with me. But when I looked around for her, she was gone. I swam back in the direction I'd come from but couldn't find her. When I surfaced, she was nowhere in sight. Then I spotted some bubbles on the surface, about twenty feet away. I dove down and swam through a thick patch of bull kelp, when I finally found her." His voice breaks. He looks down at his hands and clears his throat. "She was unconscious with a long piece of kelp wrapped several times around her leg, and fin. The kelp was wound tight. It took me some time to cut her free." He shakes his head. "Too long."

His story matches what he told the emergency dispatcher. Ethan unfolds the map of Jack Block Park he printed off before leaving the homicide unit. He slides it toward Carr.

"Could you show us where Chelsea was when you found her?"

Carr's attorney places his unnaturally tan hand on his client's shoulder. "It's okay if you don't remember."

Carr pulls the map in front of him. "I remember."

"This is only a best guess from my client's recollection of a traumatic event."

"Understood." Ethan watches Carr point to a spot on the water near a floating wharf.

"It was around here. A couple hundred yards from shore. There's a big shelf there that drops to about a hundred feet or so."

Ethan withdraws a pen from his pocket and marks the map after Carr slides it back toward him.

"Again, he's guessing."

Ethan ignores the attorney's remark. "Did she not have a knife of her own?"

"She did." Carr keeps his eyes on his hands. "But I noticed it wasn't in her holster at the hospital. She must've dropped it trying to free herself."

Ethan casts a sideways glance at his partner. They would need to send divers down from the Harbor Unit to see if they could recover it.

Jonah leans forward in his chair. "How much time passed, do you think, between when you last saw her and found her unconscious?"

He sighs. When he looks up at the detectives there are tears in his eyes. "I don't know.... Less than ten minutes. I think. I pulled her to shore as quickly as I could. There was no one on the beach, so I sprinted to my car to get my phone to call 911. I ran back to where I'd left Chelsea as I made the call."

"And you gave her CPR until the medics arrived?" Jonah asks.

They'd requested Chelsea's medical reports from the first responders and Bayside Hospital but hadn't yet received them when they left to interview Carr. They'd have to check when they returned to the department if the records matched his story.

"When I checked, she still had a weak pulse. So, I gave her mouth-to-mouth until the ambulance got there. By the time they got her breathing tube in, her pulse was gone, though."

Carr's chin quivers, and Ethan admires his acting skills as the billionaire stares out the windows at the lake.

"You never stated *why* you're opening an investigation into Chelsea's death," Carr's attorney says.

Jonah focuses his attention on Carr as he answers. "Chelsea's parents have come forward saying that Chelsea was planning to file for divorce this week, and that she had photographic evidence of you with Mason Hachette and two underage girls. You had quite the reasons to want her dead."

"That's enough." The attorney raises a hand in the air. "My client agreed to be cooperative. Not harassed. I won't have him respond to wild, unsubstantiated rumors based on hearsay."

Carr scoffs. "Oh, come on! Yeah, I knew Hachette. So did practically everyone in those circles of LA. That doesn't make me guilty of anything. I wasn't aware of any underage girls at Hachette's parties. But maybe you should ask the governor of California? He went to a lot more than I—"

"Stop talking!"

Carr gapes at his attorney's outburst, and Ethan wastes no time asking the next question while Carr is seemingly in the mood to share.

"How does a former competitive freediver, who could once hold her breath for seven minutes, swim through a thick patch of bull kelp without considering the risks of entanglement, then panic, only to further entangle herself until she passes out?"

While he and Jonah waited for Carr's attorney to arrive, Ethan watched a video of Chelsea's record-breaking freedive on his phone. After diving to a depth of three hundred feet, Ethan watched in amazement as she effortlessly pulled herself to the surface while holding her breath for over three minutes.

"Don't answer that." Carr's attorney turns and points his finger at Ethan. "That's enough. My client is *grieving*. Don't make us sue the department for emotional damages." He stands from the table. "I'll see you out."

"She was abusing opiates again," Carr says before the detectives get up. "The stress of our separation probably only made it worse."

His attorney leans over and whispers something in Carr's ear, but he waves him away.

"I had a prescription of oxycodone left over from a dental procedure in my bathroom cabinet. After Chelsea moved out, it was gone. She took it with her, I'm sure." He exhales a heavy sigh. "I'm guessing she took a few pills before we went diving yesterday."

Ethan and Jonah exchange a look. Carr's attorney strides around the table, signaling the meeting is over, but Ethan makes no move to get up.

"Did you see her take pills yesterday?" He rests his elbows on the polished wood table.

Carr shakes his head. "She'd been clean for a while. But I suspected she was using again before we separated. I could tell. She denied it when I confronted her about it, which was part of the reason she moved out."

"She had a problem with opiates before?" Jonah asks.

"Chelsea got into a party scene in LA a few years ago. *The wrong crowd,* as they say. She was taking several pills a day by the time I finally convinced her to go to rehab last year." His eyes brim with tears. He looks up at the ceiling. "I should've gotten to her sooner. I can't believe she's..." His voice cracks, and he brings a hand to his mouth.

Ethan thinks of the photos of Carr with underage girls that Chelsea was said to have on her phone. *She wasn't the only one mixed up in the wrong crowd. If that's even true.* "Did you say anything to the emergency responders about Chelsea possibly having drugs in her system?"

Carr shakes his head. "I was in shock. And she seemed fine before we went into the water. It didn't dawn on me until after she—" He exhales out his mouth. "After she died that she might've taken some before we went diving."

Carr's attorney steps closer, stopping inches from Ethan's side. "This interview is *over*. My client is distressed, and he's been more than helpful." He motions for the detectives to stand. "Let's go."

"We need you to surrender Chelsea's phone," Ethan says. "And the keys to her Belltown apartment."

"Do you have a warrant?" the attorney asks.

Jonah reaches inside his suit pocket. "We do." He extends the folded paper toward Carr's attorney who snatches it out of his hands.

He looks over the warrant with a frown. "I'll bring them to your car. As soon as you two see yourselves out."

Carr covers his face with his hands, and it takes all of Ethan's willpower to extinguish the image of them traveling down Sloane's back. Ethan keeps his eyes trained on Carr, his shoulders heaving with each dramatic sob, as he pushes back his chair.

"I loved her so much," Carr manages to say between sobs.

The attorney makes a show of impatience with a deep sigh as he gestures toward the open doorway. Ethan looks back at Carr before following Jonah out of the room. If he learned one thing from their interview, it was this: the app founder is almost as good an actor as Sloane.

Chapter 23

Sloane moves her salad around with a plastic fork in the ER breakroom, tuning out the upbeat chatter from the two nurses and medical resident at the other end of the table. She hadn't slept a minute the night before. Instead, she spent the night tossing and turning, trying to force the images of Brody—and his dead wife—from her mind. She doesn't feel like eating even though she skipped breakfast that morning, not wanting to risk bumping into Ethan in the kitchen.

Laughter breaks out from a pretty blonde nurse fresh out of nursing school, whose name escapes Sloane. Sloane glances in the nurse's direction and sees the resident showing her something on his phone. She strains to read the nurse's name badge that's clipped to her scrubs. *Rachel.* Her heart sinks. Of course, it is. Sloane looks away, willing herself to eat a bite of tasteless iceberg lettuce.

The breakroom door swings open. She turns to see Logan striding toward her.

"Hey." He leans his hand on the chair beside her.

Sloane has yet to apologize for yelling at him yesterday about the Narcan, but he seems to have forgiven her.

"Sorry to interrupt, but I wanted to clarify an order you wrote for the patient in trauma room five, Daniel Salazar.

"He was in the motorcycle accident," Logan adds, seeing the look of confusion on Sloane's face.

"Oh, right." Sloane sets down her fork. "Sure."

"You wrote the Epi 1:1,000 to be given IV. But from the dosage, I'm guessing you wanted it to be IM."

"I did?"

"Yeah."

She leans back against her chair as a twist forms in her gut. She's never made a medication error before. "Good catch. Sorry, yes. I meant IM."

Although, they both knew it was more than a good catch. If he hadn't caught her mistake, it could have put the patient into V-tach. Or worse, V-fib.

He nods.

"Go ahead and give it IM. I'll change the order."

"Okay, thank you."

Sloane rubs the sides of her temples after Logan turns for the door. *You've got to get it together.*

"Chelsea Carr's death is all over my feed."

Sloane shoots a glance at the young blonde nurse holding up her phone. With her other hand she digs inside a bag of Cheetos, even though she can't be more than a size two.

"I didn't realize she was so involved with the Children's Cancer Society because her sister died of leukemia at the age of sixteen." Rachel looks at Sophie, the nurse sitting across from her. "Did you?"

Sophie shakes her head. "No. But I watched a clip this morning of Chelsea saying she wanted to have a big family someday. So sad."

Sloane sits up straight, remembering Brody's words in her ear while he draped his arm across her breasts in the bathtub. *Chelsea hates kids.*

"Her poor parents, losing their second daughter," Sophie adds.

"And her husband..." The blonde presses her palms against the table and leans forward. "Did you see him yesterday? He was so devasted. It was heartbreaking. I wanted to give him a hug."

Sophie laughs. "I bet you did."

Sloane feels heat rise to her face.

The blonde laughs. "Seriously, though. That poor guy."

"Think he'll find his next wife on that dating app he created?" the resident asks.

"I better join just in case." Rachel smirks before stuffing several Cheetos into her mouth at once.

Sloane's chair scrapes against the linoleum when she pushes it back, causing the three heads at the other end of the table to jerk in her direction.

"Why can't you have a little respect? A woman *died*."

Rachel's jaw drops open at Sloane's outburst. "Dr. Marks, we were just—"

"It's a *tragedy*. Not a race to see who can get with her widower first." Sloane slams her chair into the table, causing her fork to slip off her salad bowl. "What's wrong with you?"

The three of them exchange glances before returning their wide-eyed stares to Sloane. Sloane turns for the door and realizes she's practically hyperventilating. *Calm down. You're losing it.*

She pauses after putting her hand on the door handle and turns. "I'm sorry. Yesterday was a rough day, and I didn't sleep well last night."

Her coworkers offer no respon... ...akroom.
She strides down the corridor and h... ...here
Chelsea died. How long will it be befo...
room and not think about Chelsea? And t...

Chapter 24

Sloane pulls the wilting bouquet of roses from Ethan out of the vase and lays them on the kitchen island, needing a distraction so she's not tempted to check her phone. She hasn't checked her news feed since early that morning—when she was bombarded with articles about Chelsea. Thankfully, Brody hasn't tried to contact her. Thinking of him pretending not to know her while putting on an act of the grieving husband makes her sick.

She stares at the flames flickering in the gas fireplace on the far wall of her living room while she fills the vase with fresh water. When she shuts off the water, she hears the hum of the garage door closing.

She sets the vase on the counter as Ethan walks into the kitchen.

"You're home early." She works to sound relaxed as she mentally sifts through the reasons he would come home in the middle of day, none of which are good.

He takes a seat on one of the bar stools. "So are you. I went to the hospital, but they said you'd left for the day."

"Oh." She tries to ignore the guilt that stabs at her chest. "Yeah, I um...wasn't feeling well so they sent me home."

She's never left a shift early before in her entire career. Her eyes meet Ethan's, and she realizes Ethan knows this as well as she does. She sticks a few healthier-looking roses back into the vase, worried that Ethan will interpret her coming home early as guilt. She needs to make sure he sees it as guilt over her affair, not helping Brody Carr murder his wife.

Ethan runs his hand up the back of his short dark hair. "I got a new case." He leans his elbows onto the quartz countertop. "Chelsea Carr's parents have come forward saying that she had photographic evidence her husband was doing a lot of partying with Mason Hachette and underage girls in LA. Photos of Carr and Hachette have already surfaced online, but we're hoping to extract more off her phone."

Sloane rests her hands against the counter to steady herself. Mason Hachette was an extremely wealthy financier who had recently been in the news after his arrest over sexual abuse charges related to minors. She remembers seeing a photo of Brody with Hachette when she searched Brody's name online a couple months back. At the time, she hadn't thought much of it. Hachette was a socialite, and photos of him with countless celebrities surfaced after his arrest.

"They separated quietly," Ethan continues, his eyes piercing hers as he studies her reaction. "But Chelsea told her parents she wouldn't stay quiet any longer. She hired a divorce attorney and was planning to make her accusations public after she filed."

The few bites of lunch she had creep up the back of Sloane's throat. Any lingering doubts she had about Brody killing Chelsea are now gone. She wants to scream. *Underage girls?* How could she have been so stupid? *Brody wanted Chelsea out of the picture so he wouldn't go to prison. And he's brought me into it.*

Her phone rings atop the counter. Ethan's eyes follow hers toward the sound. Seeing it is Brody, she swipes *Ignore*. Her heart pounds, making a mental note to block his number. It's the first time he's tried to contact her since Chelsea died. *What the hell is he doing calling me when he's under investigation for murder?*

Sloane lifts her gaze to Ethan's, who is still staring at her phone, feeling suddenly exposed. She blinks back the tears that invade her eyes. She feels sick. She needs to lie down. But she can't fall apart in front of Ethan.

When Ethan's eyes meet hers, there is no trace of the pain that filled them last night. Only a malice-laced suspicion.

He interlaces his fingers. "I got the medical report from Bayside Hospital and saw you were the doctor who pronounced Chelsea dead."

Sloane swallows. "Yes, I—I told you last night."

"Yeah, I know." He leans forward. "Was there any indication that Chelsea had drugs in her system? Like opiates?"

Her chest wall freezes as she starts to inhale. The room spins. She recounts yelling at Logan when he asked about giving Narcan. "No. Why?"

A shiver runs down her arms as her husband stares at her in silence.

She jumps at the chime of Ethan's ringtone. He keeps his eyes on her while he pulls the phone out of his suit jacket pocket.

"Ethan—"

He raises a finger in the air as he puts the phone to his ear. "Hey, Jonah." Ethan slides off the barstool and moves into the living room to take the call.

Looking at her phone, Sloane swears under her breath. She grabs another bunch of roses and arranges them in the vase, trying to look busy while she strains to hear what Ethan is saying. But Jonah is doing most of the talking.

Brody's phone records. They would prove she and Brody were having an affair. And that she lied to Ethan about it being over before Chelsea died. She remembers Brody's text only hours before Chelsea was brought to the ER. *When can I see you again?*

Had Ethan already seen the phone records? Is that why he came home? To confront her?

Sloane feels a prick in her finger when she lifts the last bunch of roses from the counter. As soon as Ethan's off the phone, she'll convince him she was telling the truth. That she already ended things with Brody, which was why she didn't reply when he texted her hours before Chelsea died.

She has to get him on her side.

"Okay, I'll be right there," she hears Ethan say.

He could be going to interview Brody right now. She's frozen in place as she watches Ethan move across the room, keeping his phone to his ear.

Blood drips onto the white quartz from her finger. She swears, remembering the prick from the rose, and runs her hand under cold water from the sink.

"Sloane, I gotta go!" Ethan calls from the hallway to their garage. "Don't wait up, I'll be home late."

"Ethan, *wait!*"

She hears the door to the garage close as she shuts off the water. She wraps her finger in a paper towel and rushes out of the kitchen.

"Ethan!"

When she opens the garage door, Ethan's car is already gone. She leans against the doorframe, staring at the empty side of the garage before going inside.

Brody's not going to give up our affair, she tells herself. He's smarter than that. He'll have an attorney. The best money can buy, who won't let him say a word.

But what if Ethan presses him? Brody has to know they'll go through his phone records and learn everything he has to hide. She saw the way Ethan looked at her in the kitchen moments ago. He doesn't trust her. And why should he? She made sure he couldn't. She can't expect Ethan not to push Brody to admit their affair, even in front of Jonah.

If Brody confesses to Ethan and his new partner, the whole department will soon know about their affair. It would be out of Ethan's hands. Being the doctor who pronounced Chelsea dead, Sloane would likely be the next one brought in for questioning.

She grabs her phone off the counter. She paces the kitchen as she waits for Ethan to answer. *Pick up.* It goes to voicemail after the third ring.

"Ethan, call me back. I need to know you're on my side."

She sinks onto the barstool that Ethan was just sitting in and cradles her head in her hands. She can't trust Brody not to tell Ethan in front of Jonah. He's a man with a lot to lose, and he's facing more than just murder charges.

She climbs off the stool and calls Ethan again as she moves through her living room. It goes to voicemail a second time. She stops and stares out her front window, letting her phone fall to her side. The sky is gray, but there's still a good hour of daylight left.

She lifts her phone, wondering if she should call Brody to warn him not to say anything to Ethan about her in front of Jonah. But that would show up in his phone records, and how would that look, especially to Ethan?

Chapter 25

A light mist falls as Sloane jogs down the sidewalk away from her house. It's been years since she exercised outside of a gym, and the cool, damp air feels good inside her lungs. She needed to get out of the house, clear her mind.

From this proximity, her neighborhood has a slightly unfamiliar feel to it. She usually only sees it from the car—leaving for the hospital before dawn and getting home after sunset. The leaves on the deciduous trees have changed from emerald to bright mustard and crimson. She takes in the neatly trimmed hedges and occasional imported palm that line her street and tries not to dwell on the fact that Ethan hasn't called her back.

She looks at the view of Elliott Bay—the same waters where Chelsea drowned—beyond the bottom of the hill, still visible in the waning daylight, as she jogs between homes. She wonders if she should try calling him again. Instead, she keeps pressing one foot in front of the other. Ethan's probably already with Jonah on their way to interview Brody.

She barely notices the black Maserati that pulls to the curb beside her. She lifts her gaze to the large weeping willow swaying from the breeze in front of the Tudor home to her left.

A car door closes. Seconds later, she feels a hand on her shoulder. She whips around and shrieks when she recognizes the man standing before her. Her knees buckle as she starts to run backward.

"Sloane!"

She falls, tearing the knee of her leggings against the sidewalk. Brody leans over and grabs her arms.

"Let me help you."

She swallows back her revulsion as she allows him to help pull her to her feet. A sedan slows as it rolls past them. Her eyes dart in the car's direction. Brody flashes the car a smile as if to say *all good here*, while she takes a step back.

"Are you *following* me?"

"I just need to talk to you. You didn't answer my call." He waits for the car to speed up before he moves toward her. "Chelsea's death is being investigated by the police."

Because you killed her to cover up your affairs with underage girls. "I know—Ethan is the one leading it. Which is why you can't call me!"

The mist turns into a full-on rain shower. The sound of droplets splattering atop the street fills the air.

"Yes, I already had a nice chat with him and his partner earlier this morning."

She feels a lurch in her stomach, thinking about Brody and Ethan in the same room, squaring off across a small interview table. *Ethan had already spoken to Brody before he came home.* "Did you—"

"Don't worry, I didn't tell him about us." He steps toward her. "Look, I know you're scared. I'm scared. But I did it for us. Chelsea was going to make my life hell. This was the only way for us to be together."

Branches from the weeping willow sway above their heads. Brody grabs her hand. She resists the urge to recoil from his touch.

"I thought about what you said in the bathtub the other night. About Ethan dying in the line of duty."

Sloane's mouth falls open. She lowers her voice, even though they're alone on the street. "I wasn't talking about *murder!*" She pulls her hand away, unable to stand his touch any longer. "Ethan's going to pull your phone records, and he'll see our affair," she adds. "But I—"

"He's not going to find our calls." Rainwater drips from his brown waves. "The phone I used to communicate with you isn't registered in my name. There's no record linking me to that number. I only use it to talk to you and my attorneys. Don't worry. We would both look guilty if we're found out, but I'll make sure that doesn't happen."

Is he threatening her? She narrows her eyes. "What do you mean *both?*"

"Well, you were the one who pronounced her dead. It looks a little premeditated when you think about it. I know it *wasn't* on your part. But tell me, did you really do *everything* you could to revive her?"

She thinks about Logan asking to give Narcan.

Brody smiles. "That's what I thought."

She gapes at him. "Of course, I did!"

He tilts his head to the side and shrugs. "If you say so."

He puts his hands on her shoulders, and Sloane resists the urge to shake them away. Brody has to believe she's on his side. The evidence of their affair could extend beyond phone records.

"You're going to hear some unpleasant things about me, which is what Chelsea wanted—to ruin my life. But don't believe it."

Headlights turn into a driveway across the street.

"It's all lies," he continues. "The guy you've gotten to know these last few months, and spent last weekend with, that's the real me. We're in this together, you and me."

She takes a step toward him. "I know we are. I just wish we were on the other side of this already."

The driver gets out of the car across the street and glances in their direction, before walking up his drive toward the pre-war home.

Brody lowers his hands to his sides. "We will be soon." He waits for the man across the street to disappear inside the house before continuing. "I know it's bad they aren't treating Chelsea's death as an accident, but they won't be able to prove otherwise. Maybe Ethan taking the case is a good thing. You can help convince him of my innocence, tell him how genuinely distraught I was at the hospital yesterday. You see a lot of grieving spouses." He steps back. "I mean, it's not like he suspects anything about us. Right?"

Goosebumps form on Sloane's arms beneath her wet running jacket as she shakes her head.

Brody waves his hand through the air. "Of course, he doesn't. You said he's never even home. So, here's what we'll do."

Sloane glances across the street.

Brody closes the small gap between them. "Find out as much as you can about the investigation and keep me informed. We'll stay one step ahead."

Sloane nods. "Okay. And you'll make sure Ethan doesn't find any evidence of our affair?"

"Of course. Once they've ruled it an accident, you can leave Ethan. And we can be free to start our life together. A family." He brings his hand to her chin, and it takes all her willpower not to spit in his face.

"Don't call me for now. It's too risky; Ethan might see it. I'll get another phone. Send you a text so you have the number." She braces for Brody to kiss her, but he backs away.

"Everything's going to be fine, love."

Sloane wants to scoff at his words as she watches him stride through the rain toward his Maserati. "Brody?"

He looks over his shoulder when he reaches his driver's door.

"Stay safe."

A smile plays at his lips as repulsion slithers down her spine. "They're not going to get me, Sloane. I love you."

After he climbs into his car, Sloane breaks into a run. In the street beside her, the Maserati makes a U-turn before speeding away down the neighborhood street. Sloane watches Brody's car disappear around a bend and picks up her pace.

Brody might think he's invincible, but he doesn't know Ethan. There's no way he's going to let Brody get away with Chelsea's murder. Sloane has no doubt Ethan is already sure of Brody's guilt. But is he sure of hers?

Chapter 26

Ethan's leg jiggles beneath his desk. He clicks through photos of Brody Carr with Mason Hachette that were attached to a recent news article, while he waits for the FBI investigator who brought charges against Hachette to return his call.

Carr denied knowing the passcode for Chelsea's phone, so they'd had to use her fingerprint to unlock it before sending it to TESU, their technical electronic support unit. No incriminating photos of Carr were found after the initial data extraction of Chelsea's phone and laptop, which Ethan suspects Carr deleted after Chelsea died. TESU was still in the process of trying to recover any deleted files from her cloud storage account.

After Ethan went home to see Sloane's reaction to the investigation into Chelsea's death, he and Jonah conducted a search of Chelsea's Belltown apartment, along with a CSI team, which hadn't yielded much. Contrary to her husband's claims, there were no drugs.

Thinking about Carr carrying on an affair with Sloane makes Ethan want to puke. He recalls the look on her face when he told her what spurred them to open the investigation. *Was she disappointed? Or just disturbed?* It drives him crazy that he doesn't know her well enough to be able to tell the difference. *How badly had she fallen for that rich, sadistic prick?*

How can he even be sure it's over between them? Hopefully, he'll find out when he gets Carr's phone records, which he needs to make sure he sees before Jonah does.

Ethan hasn't returned Sloane's calls. He replays her frantic-sounding voicemail in his head. *I need to know that you're on my side.* She has a right to be worried after getting mixed up in an affair with Carr, but it's *why* she's worried that bothers him.

His desk phone rings, jarring him from his thoughts. Seeing the California area code, he lifts the receiver before it rings a second time. "Detective Marks."

"Hi, this is Agent Campos from the Los Angeles FBI," a female voice says. "I got your voicemail, about Brody Carr."

"Thanks for calling. I'm investigating the death of his wife, Chelsea. According to her parents, she was in possession of photos of Carr on Mason Hachette's yacht with underage girls. We're still in the process of recovering the images, but I was wondering if Carr came up in your investigation of Hachette."

"He did, but after Amelia Vasquez was killed, we didn't have enough evidence to charge him."

Ethan recognizes the name.

"You might recall from the news that Amelia Vasquez was killed in what we believe was a staged home invasion the night before she was set to testify against Hachette."

"I remember. So, you think it's probable that Carr's wife had photos of him with underage girls?"

"Very, although we were never able to get our hands on any. My guess is that Amelia is who sent Chelsea those photos. They were in the modeling industry together, and Amelia attended several of Hachette's parties. After she was killed, several of our key witnesses, who were underage girls, were too afraid to cooperate with the investigation. Their money and power make men like Hachette and Carr feel they can get away with anything. And sadly, sometimes they do. We had enough evidence to convict Hachette, but I'm afraid that when it comes to Carr we do not. At least, not yet."

Ethan stares at the photo still up on his screen and clenches his jaw.

"Let me know if you find anything that could be useful to us in nailing that bastard," she adds.

"I will. Thanks for your help."

"Carr's phone records came in," Jonah says from behind him as soon as Ethan hangs up. "I printed them off." He slaps a thick stack of papers onto his desk.

Ethan stares at the records, feeling a constriction in his chest. He meant to get to them before Jonah did.

Ethan swivels his chair. "I'll take those."

"No, I got it." Jonah plops into his seat. "You leave here later than me every night. I'm sure my eyes are fresher than yours." He flashes Ethan a grin. "I gotta pull my weight around here, so you don't go requesting a new partner."

A knot forms in Ethan's stomach as Jonah turns his attention to Carr's cell records. He extends his hand toward the stack. "Really, it's fine. I like doing this stuff. And my eyes are fine. I got a good night's sleep last night," he lies.

"You sure?"

"Yeah." Ethan tries to hide his relief as Jonah lifts the stack off his desk.

"Okay." Jonah rolls back his chair. "Then I'll go see if Chelsea's divorce attorney can speak with me before I meet the Harbor Unit at Jack Block Park." Jonah stands. "What time are we meeting with Chelsea's parents?"

"They should be here by six."

"I'll be back by then. McKinnon said it's a fourteen-hour flight. That's a long haul."

Ethan is already scanning the first page for Sloane's number as Jonah steps out of the unit. For once, he's glad Rachel is no longer his partner. While Ethan found it more efficient to split up and address different things simultaneously, Rachel preferred to investigate every detail of their cases together. She argued it was more thorough, that two pairs of eyes were always better than one. She was afraid they would miss something by addressing things solo, but Ethan didn't agree. Catching killers is always time sensitive and doing everything together only slowed things down. It was the one thing they constantly disagreed on.

Skimming through Carr's phone records looking for Sloane's number, he's grateful Jonah is new enough to homicide and he still follows Ethan's lead. The date on Carr's phone records starts two months ago, and he realizes he has no idea how long Sloane's affair with Carr has been going on. He flips to the next page.

There's no way he can keep Sloane's affair a secret, he knows that. He has to tell McKinnon after he goes through the records. Then, he'll get kicked off the case—and the whole department will know why. He'll have to trust that Jonah will do what's necessary to ensure that the rich asshole gets what's coming to him.

But first, he needs to know how long it was going on. How often Sloane was communicating with her sex-offender lover. Ethan flips to the third page, still not having seen Sloane's number on Carr's call logs.

He feels only slight relief that the affair has been going on less than two months. The shorter the fling, the less likely it seems Sloane could have been involved in the murder of Carr's wife. If the case goes to trial, there will be no way to keep the affair out of the media. Even with Sloane wanting his forgiveness, he doubts their marriage will survive it.

By the bottom of the fourth page, he still hasn't spotted Sloane's number. Unable to take it any longer, he digs through the pages until he finds the date of Sloane's hospital award ceremony. He runs his finger down the list of numbers called that day.

There was a two-minute call at 3:16 p.m. and not another call until 7:58 p.m. that night. Ethan stares at the date at the top of the page. He doesn't have it wrong. And it had to have been between five and six p.m. when he heard Sloane on the phone in their bathroom. *So, where is it?*

He skims through the text messages from that day. If they were talking on the phone, and sleeping together, they had to be texting too. But there was nothing to or from Sloane's number. Ethan scans the next several pages. Still nothing.

He lifts his phone from the desk and calls Jonah, who answers on the second ring.

"Hey," Ethan says. "Are these all the phone records from Brody Carr?"

"That's the only cell phone account in his name. I double checked. Why?"

Ethan puts his hand to his forehead, staring at the papers splayed across his desk. It would be better for Sloane if they don't find them, but he needs to know. Plus, if Carr had an unregistered number, there was likely much more damning evidence on it than his affair with Ethan's wife. "I guess I expected a guy like that to have more than one number, you know?"

"If he does, there's no record of it."

"Huh. Okay, thanks. I'll keep looking through these. Let me know what you learn from the divorce attorney. And how it goes with the dive team."

Ethan hangs up and goes through each page again. Certain that Sloane's number isn't anywhere in Carr's cell records, he rubs his eyes. He thinks about her phone ringing when he came home earlier, and how quick she was to decline the call. His desk phone rings, bringing him back to the present.

"Detective Marks."

"Ethan, it's Pete."

He recognizes the medical examiner's gravelly voice.

"I wanted to let you know I'm sending over my official autopsy report for Chelsea Carr. We'll have to wait the usual four to six weeks for toxicology, and I've left her manner of death as undetermined. I didn't find anything that is inconsistent with an accidental drowning. There's a ligature mark around her left leg, but it is consistent with being wound in bull kelp, like her husband said."

Ethan leans back in his chair.

"So, whether I'm able to make a final determination on her death being either accidental or homicide will likely depend on your investigation."

"Thanks, Pete."

After hanging up, Ethan stares at his computer screen, which has now gone dark. Carr is good at hiding things, and he went to some trouble to keep his and Sloane's communication hidden. Getting their hands on it might be the only way to prove his affairs with underage girls, and his motive for killing Chelsea.

They would need a search warrant for Carr's Medina property if they were going to have a chance at finding Carr's unregistered phone. With the statements from Chelsea's parents, along with her divorce attorney, they should be able to get a judge to approve one.

Unfortunately, uncovering Brody's secrets would also bring Sloane's to light. He thinks back to his wife's earlier reaction in their kitchen. Was it a coincidence that Sloane pronounced Carr's wife dead? Or something more? Brody Carr, Ethan knows, is a man with much more to hide than an affair.

But what about Sloane?

Chapter 27

Ethan walks out of the conference room and spots Jonah returning to their cubicle at the other end of the hall.

"Chelsea's parents just got here," Ethan says when he gets closer. "They're in the conference room." When he met them, Ethan felt a burst of sympathy. They looked exhausted, and their tired eyes were flooded with grief. "Did you get the knife booked into evidence?"

Jonah hangs his coat over the back of his chair. He called Ethan less than an hour ago, saying the harbor unit's dive team recovered a knife not far from the location Carr had marked on Ethan's map.

"Yeah, just now. I'm having them send it to the Latent Print Unit even though there's probably no prints after it's been submerged in water for two days."

"How did it go with the attorney?"

"Not bad, but not great." Jonah speaks in a low tone, ensuring Chelsea's parents couldn't overhear, even though they were at the other end of the hall. "Chelsea only had a preliminary meeting with her. She paid a retainer and was planning to file for divorce this week. Chelsea hadn't shared many specifics—just that her husband had been unfaithful. She denied there ever being any domestic violence, but she did hint at having some damning evidence that she could use against him in the divorce proceedings. But she didn't say what it was."

Ethan crosses his arms. "Did she have any idea why Chelsea would go freediving with him?"

"Chelsea told her attorney she was going to tell Carr in person before she filed for divorce, which her attorney advised her was a bad idea. Chelsea said he'd been pleading with her not to divorce him until his latest business acquisition was finalized, but Chelsea said she couldn't wait any longer. So, maybe she went with him to break the news about her decision to divorce, and he killed her. Carr had more reasons to want his wife dead than I can even count."

"Uh-huh."

"Did you find any evidence of an affair on his phone records?"

Ethan shakes his head. "Not so far."

"You okay?"

Ethan looks up, realizing he was staring at the floor. Jonah studies him as he waits for Ethan's response.

"Yeah." He clears his throat. "Pete called earlier and said, so far, Chelsea's autopsy doesn't suggest anything other than an accidental drowning. She has a ligature mark around her leg, but it's consistent with Carr's account that she got tangled in bull kelp."

"Hmm. Maybe what we learn from Chelsea's parents can help us prove otherwise." Jonah slaps him on the shoulder. "Ready to talk to them?"

❦

Ethan notes the striking resemblance Chelsea's mother, Tanya, bears to her daughter as she sits across from him at the conference table.

The tall, slender woman shares the same high cheekbones Ethan has seen in Chelsea's photos. He guesses Tanya looked nearly identical to Chelsea when she was younger.

She locks her red and puffy eyes with Ethan's. "Chelsea found out about Brody's taste for underage girls a few months ago. After Mason Hachette was arrested. An ex-model friend of hers sent her a photo of Brody and the young girl on Hachette's boat." She fingers the untouched Styrofoam cup of coffee Ethan brought her earlier. "At first, Brody denied it. Said she had no proof of any wrongdoing, and his lawyers would dispute it if Chelsea ever made any claims. And after her friend was murdered, Chelsea got too scared to bring it up again. She and Brody separated, and Chelsea moved into their condo in Belltown." She stares into her coffee cup. "But Brody convinced her to keep quiet about their separation until after the acquisition of Crush was finalized."

A look passes between Ethan and Jonah on the other side of the table. Her story matches up perfectly with Chelsea's divorce attorney. Ethan read about the acquisition online earlier that day. Carr purchased the trendy dating app for nearly a billion dollars last month, and the acquisition was projected to increase his fortune by much more than that.

"Then, a few weeks ago, Chelsea got a private message on one of her social media accounts," her father, Don, says. The bags under his eyes make him look even more worse for wear than his wife. "Of an underage girl sitting on Brody's lap, hardly wearing anything, mate!" A tear slips down his face as he shakes his head. "Her face was blurred out. And when Chelsea tried to reply to the message, the sender's account was closed." He shakes his head. "The young girl is probably terrified to speak out against these rich wankers."

"Do you know which social media account this was?" Ethan asks.

Tanya shakes her head before putting her hand on her husband's arm. "No. But we warned Chelsea not to say anything to Brody about the photo. Told her to take the image to the police. She was planning to do it this week, after she filed for divorce."

Chelsea's father leans forward, pressing his elbows into the table. "But then, last Friday, she and Brody got into a huge argument over the phone, and she let it slip that he could be looking at prison time." His jaw goes slack as fresh tears well in his eyes.

Tanya looks at Jonah. "We didn't know she agreed to see him yesterday. We would've tried to stop her if we did. We know how manipulative Brody can be. Conniving. Smooth. He's so used to getting what he wants."

Like my wife. Ethan notes Tanya's chin quivers as she purses her lips.

"Chelsea was always too trusting." Her father covers his eyes with his hand. "I knew it was going to get her into trouble someday. Just not like this." His voice breaks.

His wife reaches for his hand. "Even after everything, I think in some strange way, she was still in love with the sick bastard."

Ethan tears his gaze from the grieving couple and stares out at the lights of the Seattle waterfront through the windows beyond them. *Maybe Chelsea wasn't the only one.*

Chapter 28

Sloane meets Ethan in the kitchen after she hears him come through the garage. He never returned her calls. The hours passed like years since she got back from her run. Ethan pulls a beer from the fridge and leans against the counter.

"Hey," she says.

He looks exhausted. She's dying to press him about the investigation, to know Brody was telling the truth about the phone records.

He opens his beer and locks his tired eyes with hers. "Tell me you had nothing to do with Chelsea's death."

"What do you mean?"

His face hardens. "You were having an affair with a man who *killed* his wife."

"We don't know that for su—"

"He killed her, Sloane!" Ethan raises his hands in the air. "And then, out of all the doctors in Seattle, *you* were the one who pronounced his wife dead."

"I tried to revive her! I had no idea Brody was going to do that. I obviously had no idea who he really was!"

"It's not me you should be worried about convincing."

Sloane's blood runs cold. "What are you talking about?" Had Brody lied about the phone records? "Has our affair already come up?"

"Not yet." Ethan moves around the kitchen island. "But it would look better if you come forward before it comes to light."

Brody's threat echoes in her mind as Sloane leans against the fridge. *If we're found out, we'll* both *look guilty.* "It's going to look bad, whether I come forward or not at this point."

He grips the back of one of the barstools, lowering his gaze to the counter. "Did anyone see you when you went to his house after your award gala? Like his staff?"

She shakes her head. "No."

"What about his house in the San Juans?"

"We were alone."

"He has security cameras at his home. Probably at his San Juan property too. I don't see us checking it now, but it's possible—"

"I could ask Brody to erase it. I'm sure he—"

"No!" Ethan swipes his hand through the air.

Sloane can't remember ever seeing him this angry.

"Do *not* communicate with him! Okay?"

She nods. "Okay."

Ethan pinches the bridge of his nose with his thumb and forefinger. "If we find the incriminating photos Chelsea presumably had, the FBI could get involved. This is..." He shakes his head. "Unbelievable. I need you to give me the phone number you've been using to call Brody. Your number didn't show up on his phone records, which means he has another phone."

"Why?" A ripple of fear crawls down her spine. If he gets a warrant for Brody's unregistered phone, she'll become an official part of the investigation. "I thought you were going to help—"

"There could be evidence on the phone records from that number, like his communication with Hachette. Or even underage girls."

"But it could also incriminate *me*." She moves toward the island. "Like you said, I was having an affair with a man who killed his wife! After Chelsea died, Brody and I pretended like we didn't know each other. Then I went on with the rest of my shift as usual." *Well, pretty much.* "If we're found out, you're right, it's not going to look good."

Ethan's knuckles blanch as he tightens his grip on her costly barstools. "I can't believe this is happening." He lowers his gaze to the countertop. "Why the hell did it have to be Brody Carr?"

Sloane bites her lip, deciding this isn't the moment to explain that, before her affair, Ethan couldn't even come home long enough to have sex when she was ovulating *and* missed both their anniversary and the most important night of her career. Not to mention that he cheated first.

There's a lot more at stake now than having the last word.

"I'm sorry," she whispers.

Ethan clenches his jaw. "I need to get some sleep." He runs his hand up the back of his head. "And think more about this in the morning."

"Good night," she says after he turns and heads for the stairs.

"Good night," he mutters.

She waits until she stops hearing his footsteps above her to retrieve the prepaid phone from her purse that she purchased with cash earlier that night. She glances at the staircase before sending a text to the number she now knows by heart. *It's me. I need to see you again.*

Chapter 29

S loane turns up the volume on the car stereo after pulling out of her neighborhood, blaring a new hit single from a local pop radio station in the hope of drowning out her thoughts. After texting Brody last night, who she has yet to hear back from, she sent Ethan his number. She hesitated before sending it, knowing that if the phone records got into the wrong hands, she could be implicated. But she can't afford to look like she's still keeping things from Ethan if they are going to get through this together.

While she feels fairly confident that Ethan will do what's necessary to protect her, she knows he won't do the same for Brody. And if Brody's arrested, what will keep him from accusing her to deflect his own guilt? She peers out at a cruise ship when she nears the end of Magnolia Bridge, unable to fathom what it would be like to be on vacation without a care in the world.

The song ends, and a female radio personality's voice fills her car.

"Breaking news this morning as new details emerge around the untimely death of freediver-turned-model, Chelsea Carr. Our sources report that Chelsea's death is now being investigated by Seattle homicide detectives, after her parents came forward accusing her husband, billionaire Brody Carr, of killing her."

Sloane's fingers tighten around the steering wheel.

"According to the model's parents, she was planning to divorce Brody Carr after learning he'd attended yacht parties with several underage girls that were hosted by Brody's friend, convicted sex offender, Mason Hachette. Seattle homicide detectives have refused to comment at this point other than to say the investigation is ongoing."

Sloane feels nauseous, remembering Brody's body against hers in the bathtub, the warmth of his breath on her ear.

"I mean," her male counterpart says, "just when you think the details surrounding Chelsea Carr's death couldn't get any worse—they do."

Sloane turns off the radio. She wonders what the likelihood is that the FBI will get involved, like Ethan said. A horn blares outside her window. She turns to see a dark SUV enter the intersection, speeding toward her driver's side door. She floors the gas as she flies beneath the red light, her heart hammering against her chest. In her rearview mirror, she watches with wide eyes as the SUV skids to a stop, missing the back of her car by mere inches.

Mouth agape, she clings to the steering wheel, her chest heaving up and down. She drives a good ten miles per hour under the speed limit the rest of the way to the hospital, still shaking when she pulls into the parking garage.

She contemplates calling in sick. But at this late hour, they'd be hard pressed to find anyone to replace her. Everyone in the ER was overworked and exhausted. Evelyn turns her Escalade into the *Physician's Only* parking bay beside her, and Sloane feels a ping of guilt at the thought of abandoning her. Plus, it would only add to Brody's case if he *does* accuse her of conspiring with him to kill Chelsea—if she's out sick the days following her death.

She takes a steadying breath before opening her car door.

"Morning, sunshine." Evelyn appears behind her Porsche holding a large Starbucks. "I texted you to see if you wanted coffee."

"Oh," Sloane says. "I must have my phone on silent." She runs a hand through her hair, unable to remember if she brushed it that morning.

Evelyn's long hair is pulled back, and her eyes are puffy. While she looks sleep deprived, she also looks happy. Sloane swallows back the envy she feels creep to the surface.

Evelyn assesses her before taking a sip from her drink. "Don't take this the wrong way, but you look like crap." Evelyn elbows her as a smile forms on her lips. "You sure you're not pregnant?"

Chapter 30

E than stares at the underwater photo of Chelsea on Carr's living room wall. TESU was still working to recover any deleted images off Chelsea's phone when Ethan called them this morning. According to the data extraction technician whom he spoke with, if there *were* images deleted from her device, whoever deleted them was tech savvy enough to permanently delete them from her cloud storage. But if they were deleted in the last sixty days, the technician was hopeful they could recover them. It would just take time.

Ethan wasn't as optimistic. The app founder undoubtedly has the knowledge and resources to ensure the images won't be found. When Ethan asked if there was an option to send the phone to a private electronic forensics lab if TESU was unsuccessful, he was told that with TESU's recently upgraded technology, if they couldn't recover the images, no other lab could either.

He crosses his arms as he studies Chelsea's lean, athletic form, diving headfirst—perfectly parallel to the vertical cable attached to her ankles by a cord. From his recent research, Ethan learned that several divers die every year after becoming entangled in kelp. It was a known safety hazard amongst divers.

So how is a former competitive freediver so unaware of the dangers of diving around bull kelp? According to Carr, Chelsea was already unconscious when he reached her. But this was a woman who could once hold her breath for nearly seven minutes. Had she really panicked, further entangling herself to the point of death, while her estranged husband swam nearby, completely unaware before it was too late?

Like they presumed, the Latent Print Unit wasn't able to lift any prints off Chelsea's recovered knife, making no way to disprove Carr's account of Chelsea dropping it while trying to cut herself free.

One of the crime scene investigators assisting with the search moves past him, carrying Carr's laptop in a plastic evidence bag. The investigator's eyes follow Ethan's toward the photo. From the look on her face, Ethan guesses she is thinking the same thing: *Ironic that a woman with such power and determination would die in a recreational diving accident.*

Carr was livid when Ethan showed up at his door with a search warrant and CSI team, two hours earlier. Recalling the stunned look on the app founder's face—who obviously thought he was untouchable—when Ethan told him to surrender his phone, fills Ethan with a small sense of satisfaction. After he informed the billionaire that he couldn't be present during the search of his mansion, Carr threatened to sue him for harassment before peeling out of the drive.

Aside from the laptop and Carr's primary phone, the search hasn't turned up anything. There was no sign of a second phone, but Ethan hadn't expected him to be careless enough to leave it lying around. Carr probably took it with him when he left the house, or had given it to his attorney to hold on to during the investigation. According to Carr, Chelsea hadn't been at the home since they separated two months ago. But the laptop was what Ethan was mainly after. After being booked into evidence, it would be taken directly to TESU to see if they could extract anything that could prove Carr's guilt.

From the data TESU *was* able to extract from Chelsea's phone, along with her cell records, the estranged couple hadn't had much in the way of communication in the last two months. No threats. No mention of Carr's criminal extracurricular activities with his pal Mason Hachette. The few texts they'd exchanged could be chalked up to any couple on the brink of divorce.

"Hey, Marks."

Ethan looks away from the image of Chelsea to see Jonah moving through the living room toward him.

"Find anything?" Jonah looks beyond Ethan at the view of Lake Washington through the floor-to-ceiling windows behind him. "Wow. Not a bad view. Think I'll ever afford a place like this on my detective's salary?"

Ethan shakes his head, ignoring his partner's second question. "No. Just Carr's laptop and phone. Hopefully they will have what we need. How did it go with Carr's assistant?"

"His former assistant. When I reached out this morning to see if she'd meet with me, she said she quit after hearing the allegations against her boss. She wasn't aware of Chelsea being in possession of incriminating photos and hadn't witnessed any threats between Chelsea and Carr. But she *did* say Brody Carr was having an affair. As recent as last weekend."

Ethan feels like a rock has been dropped into his stomach.

"Carr's assistant heard him on the phone last week having an intimate conversation with a woman. And she knew it definitely wasn't Chelsea."

Ethan swallows, remembering Sloane's laughter while on the phone in the bathroom. "Does she know if Carr has a second phone?"

Jonah shakes his head. "He was in the other room, so she didn't see what phone he was using. As far as she's aware, he only has one. But Carr flew his float plane to his home on San Juan Island last weekend, and his assistant said the woman went with him."

"Did she see them?"

"No, but Carr had her order a bikini and woman's wetsuit to be delivered to his home on the island. There's a full-time caretaker who lives on the property, so he might be able to tell us more. I'm waiting for him to call me back. It would be worth interviewing this woman, if we can find out who she is. Maybe Carr shared his plan with her to get rid of his wife." Jonah cracks a smile. "He seems like the kind of guy to unload his deep, dark secrets during some late-night pillow talk."

Ethan stares out the window, picturing Sloane lying next to Brody at his island home, discussing how to get Chelsea out of the picture.

"Or maybe Carr will just give us her name." Jonah slaps Ethan on the shoulder, jarring him from his thoughts. "Unless she's underage."

Ethan turns to his partner. *She's forty-two.*

Jonah's brow furrows, seeing the look on Ethan's face. "Dude, are feeling you okay? You look... pale."

Jonah walks beside him as they move slowly through the mansion's main level. They pass by the kitchen, and Ethan's eyes settle on the barstools against the marble kitchen island. They look identical to the ones in his own home, only these are black instead of brown.

"Yeah." He lies. "I was just thinking we're going to need more to charge him with murder." Ethan's not confident they will find it. Proving motive is one thing. Proving murder is another.

He eyes the colorful underwater photographs that line one of the hallways, wondering if they were taken by Brody or Chelsea.

They reach the doorway to the master bedroom. From the bedding piled onto the bare king-size mattress, CSI has already finished with the room. Ethan steps toward the bed, too easily imagining Sloane in it, entangled with Brody.

"This guy had it all, yet it still wasn't enough."

Ethan pulls himself from his thoughts and turns toward Jonah's voice. His partner is standing near the entrance to a walk-in closet, looking pensively at a blown-up black-and-white photo of Chelsea's naked silhouette. It covers the entire wall beside the doorway.

"I mean, how do you cheat on a woman like that? This other woman he took to the San Juans must be something." Jonah glances at Ethan over his shoulder.

Before Ethan can answer, Jonah's phone rings. He checks the caller ID before putting it to his ear.

"Detective Nolan."

Ethan exhales as Jonah steps into the hall. He peers again at Carr's unmade bed before moving his attention to Chelsea's image on the wall. She can no longer speak for herself. It is up to Ethan to do it for her—and she deserves justice.

He thinks about what Jonah said before his partner's phone rang. What would justice for Chelsea mean for Sloane?

Chapter 31

The ER's automatic doors slide open seconds before two medics roll a twenty-nine-year-old woman through the entrance. Sloane steps toward the stretcher to assess the barely conscious patient, who presented with symptoms of diabetic ketoacidosis and a blood sugar registering over six hundred.

The woman starts to convulse after being rolled inside, but all Sloane can think about as she stares at her long blonde hair is Chelsea.

"Dr. Marks!"

Logan's shout jars her from her thoughts, and Sloane realizes he'd asked her a question. The woman continues to seize as Logan turns her onto her side, stabilizing her airway as the medics push her stretcher into a treatment room.

Exasperation permeates from Logan's wide eyes.

"I said, she needs Ativan! How much do you want me to give? Three milligrams or four?"

"Um." She blinks the image of Chelsea from her mind. "Four. And let's up her fluids and get another blood sugar. She may need more insulin, too."

The patient stops seizing, and Logan shoots Sloane a wary glance before hurrying to retrieve the medication.

Two hours later, Sloane moves through the same automatic doors after the end of her shift. She heads left toward the parking garage. After checking her phone, Sloane zips up her coat as a cold breeze hits her. She hasn't heard from Ethan all day. She can't stop wondering what's happening with his investigation. There weren't any news updates when she checked earlier in her shift, aside from an article headlined: *CHELSEA CARR'S MATCHMAKING HUSBAND ACCUSED OF CHEATING WITH UNDERAGE GIRLS.*

She closed out of her search without reading the article, knowing she wouldn't be able to stomach it. It would be better to get her information from Ethan anyway—if she can get him to share. Hopefully, he'll be home when she gets there.

Brody still hasn't responded to her text, and it's starting to worry her.

"Hey!"

Sloane jumps at the male voice cutting through the darkness behind her. She turns, white knuckling her bag.

"Dr. Marks!" Logan jogs toward her, wearing a hooded windbreaker over his scrubs. "Wait up!"

She exhales and lowers her bag.

"I'm already regretting picking up that overtime shift tomorrow," Logan says when he catches up to her.

"I'm surprised you agreed to come back for more after the day we had," she says.

Although every shift lately seems like the day they had.

"I should probably pick up an extra shift too," she adds.

Logan turns to her as they cross the street. "I don't think you should. I'm saying this as your friend. You really need a break."

Sloane swallows, hating that he's right. As hard as it is for her to admit it, she's bordering on unsafe.

They reach the parking garage, and Logan opens the door to the stairwell. He motions for Sloane to enter first.

"I'm sorry about earlier," she says. "I didn't sleep well last night, but I know that's no excuse."

"It's okay. But I'm worried about you."

Sloane reaches for the railing as they climb the concrete steps side by side.

"You work too much," Logan continues. "And it's getting to you."

Sloane keeps her gaze focused straight ahead. *If only that's all this was.*

"You need a few days off. Go somewhere. *Relax.* Emma and I went east of the mountains to a little town called Prosser last weekend. It's in the middle of wine country, and we stayed at this cool hotel on the river called Desert Estates."

Sloane stops when they reach the second level and reaches for the door. "You're probably right. I have the next two days off. I promise not to pick up any overtime."

"Good."

She pulls open the heavy door. "You on this level?"

He points up. "Next one."

"Okay." Sloane leans against the door, seeing her Porsche on the other side of the garage. She uses her key fob to start the engine and unlock it. "I'll see you next week. And Logan?"

He turns, halfway up the flight of stairs.

"Thank you."

He nods before continuing up the steps. Sloane exhales, watching him disappear after he rounds the top. She takes long strides toward her Porsche after hearing the metal door clang shut behind her, the sound echoing through the dimly lit garage. She scans the level. It's half-empty at this hour.

She sinks against her warm leather seat after reaching her car, reminded of her near accident this morning. She allows the relief to settle in that she doesn't have to show her face at the hospital for the next two days. She digs inside her purse to find her new prepaid phone. Still nothing from Brody.

Why not?

She thinks about texting him again but decides better of it. She needs to talk to him. Get him to erase any security footage of her at his home. And the San Juans.

Sloane watches her backup camera as she reverses out of her parking spot. "You better keep our affair to yourself, Brody Carr."

Chapter 32

Sloane keeps the radio off as she merges onto I-5 after leaving the hospital, knowing it would be quicker than driving through downtown this time of night. Still wary from her near accident that morning, she sets her cruise control at five under the speed limit. *Logan is right,* she thinks as a semi speeds past her in the adjacent lane.

She has to take control of her life. She cannot allow everything she's worked for to be taken from her because of a man. Like Crystal, who always relied on someone else to give them the life they should have had. Cars overtake her in the neighboring lane, and Sloane increases her cruise control to the speed limit. *I am not my mother.*

She thinks back to the headline about accusations against Brody from Chelsea's parents. And what Ethan said about the FBI potentially getting involved. *Maybe I should've come forward about the affair with Brody, like Ethan suggested last night.* How is it going to look if the FBI—or Ethan's partner—learns about the affair, and that she kept quiet about it?

She wonders what made Ethan ask about Chelsea having drugs in her system. If their affair comes out and Chelsea's toxicology comes back positive for opiates, it could look like she didn't do everything she could to save her. Like they planned it together. How could she prove they hadn't?

She stares at the red glow of taillights in front of her. *If only I hadn't let Evelyn take her break first.*

She drives beneath an overpass. Headlights shine into her rearview mirror, and Sloane puts on her turn signal to merge into the far right-hand lane. Before merging, she glances over her shoulder. A broad figure sits upright in her backseat.

"*Ahhh!*" Her body tenses as she makes out the familiar, wavy hairline of the man sitting behind her.

"Watch out!" Brody reaches forward for the wheel as the car speeds toward the concrete barrier at the side of the freeway.

Brody's hand closes around the steering wheel, and the car jerks to the left. Sloane's heart jumps as her Porsche swerves across three lanes of high-speed traffic. She's blinded by the several sets of headlights shining through her driver's side window as the blare of horns and screeching tires muffle her scream.

Sloane grips the wheel on either side of Brody's hand, yanking it hard to the right before they cross into the far-left lane. She throws her elbow into Brody's neck. He lets out a grunt as his hand falls away from the wheel. Sloane's breath catches in her throat as more horns erupt. Her overcorrection sends them speeding across two lanes straight at the concrete barrier again.

She pulls the wheel to the left and lets off the gas. The car straightens out when they cruise onto the shoulder, but not in time. A grinding scrape fills the car as the Porsche's passenger side slams against the barrier. Sloane lays on the brakes, throwing Brody forward between the seats.

Sloane is whipped to the side, her head smacking against the window before her seatbelt locks. Her passenger-side mirror nearly snaps off. Sloane flinches as it flaps back and forth against the windshield, causing a crack before it bounces off.

Brody holds his palms against her dash as she presses the brake to the floor. More horns resound from cars whizzing past. She flips on her hazard lights as the car slows to a stop. Brody sinks into his seat in the back. She brings her hands to her face, hyperventilating as cars zoom past, shaking the little car. Ahead of her, several tents occupy a small grassy area that separates the interstate from an onramp. A homeless man pokes his head out to assess the source of the noise.

A hand on her shoulder causes her to jump. She shrieks, having nearly forgotten Brody was in her backseat. She slaps his hand away before turning around. He puts up his palms in defense. His brown waves hang over his eyes, and Sloane sees that a red bump has formed on his temple.

"What the hell are you doing?" she screams. "You could've killed us!"

"Calm down."

"I will not calm down! How did you—" She takes a deep breath. "How'd you get back there?"

The car rattles from the wind caused by a semi cruising past them.

"I snuck in after you unlocked it. While you were turned around talking to that guy inside the stairwell. I didn't want to risk us being seen together on any hospital security cameras." He runs his fingers through his hair, pulling his hair away from his face. "I got your text, but I thought it would be better if we kept our communication face-to-face, even with your new number. Your husband's damn investigation into me is coming down hard."

Another horn blares as a sedan speeds by. Sloane is aware of her Porsche sticking out over the fog line, but there's no room to move over any farther. The other side of her car is already pressed against the concrete barrier.

"Plus, I wanted to see you." He cracks a smile.

His navy sweater is a perfect match to the ring around his hazel irises. Sloane grits her teeth, glancing out the window at the traffic zooming past.

"But we need to move. It won't look good for either of us to be seen together if the cops show up." He points out the cracked windshield. "Let's go."

He lays down again in her backseat as she sinks against her seat and tries to calm her breathing. She winces as the side of her car scrapes along the concrete again as she merges onto the freeway. But her banged-up car is the least of her problems.

Sloane eyes Brody in the rearview mirror, furious that this is how he chose to contact her. She recounts him sitting up in her backseat like something out of a horror movie before she lost control, crossing several lanes of high-speed traffic. We could've died. *What is wrong with him?*

She frowns, forcing herself to focus on why she contacted him in the first place. "Is the FBI investigating you?" When she takes the next exit off the interstate, she notices her hands are trembling.

"The FBI? Because of an old photo of me with Hachette?" He scoffs in the darkness behind her. "Did your husband tell you that? Please. If having your photo taken with Hachette was a crime, they'd be arresting practically every A-list celebrity in Hollywood. Plus, the governor of California. He was a lot closer to Hachette than I was. I barely knew him."

She pulls into the first gas station she sees and parks in an unlit bay several spots away from any other cars. Hopefully, far enough not to be spotted by anyone she knows.

Brody leans forward between the front seats. "Your husband and his partner searched my house today. Took my laptop, my phone. It's a total invasion of privacy. But they won't find anything incriminating. Sloane, Chelsea's allegations were completely unfounded. She got caught up with people who ruin themselves with their own drugs, and when they're done with that, they resent the people around them who actually made it."

Sloane turns. "Then why did you kill her?"

"So we could be together. That much should be clear." He reaches for her hand.

She fights the urge to pull away as she allows him to intertwine his fingers with hers.

"You have no idea the shitstorm she would've caused in our divorce."

Her jaw falls open before she can stop it. He talks like murder is such a reasonable alternative to divorce.

"Sloane, trust me. I know it seems bad. But there's nothing to worry about."

"Except that you killed your wife before I pronounced her dead, and now Ethan's investigating you for murder!"

"They might be able to prove motive, but no one can ever prove what happened beneath those waters is different from my account."

Her eyes meet his in the faint lights from her dash. Does he really think he's that untouchable? That he'll get away with it? It hadn't worked for Hachette. She turns and stares out the windshield, blown away by his dismissal of Chelsea's death.

"Ethan seems to think there could've been drugs in Chelsea's system. Why?"

He moves his thumb up and down hers, causing her to inwardly shiver.

"Because I told him so. It's no secret she went to rehab early last year. And if she *was* using again, it would help explain how she drowned."

Sloane turns. "Was she?"

He smirks. "I guess we'll find out when her toxicology comes back."

His note of confidence disturbs her. Sloane's eyes dart to a man leaving the convenience store before she looks back at Brody. He pulls his hand from hers and strokes the side of her face. She closes her eyes.

"Is there anything else you want to ask me? Or have we done enough talking?" He lowers his mouth to hers.

She presses her palm against his chest and pulls away. "The security footage. At your house and your San Juan Island home. If the police find that I'm on it—if *Ethan* finds that I'm on it—"

"Don't worry. I turned my security cameras off the night you came to Medina. I didn't want to give Chelsea anything she could use against me. And Ethan isn't going to check the ones at my home on San Juan Island. He'd have to get a warrant, and there's no reason to." He rests his elbow on her armrest. "Have you learned anything from Ethan about the investigation?"

She shakes her head. "Just that, as of last night, they hadn't found the incriminating photos of you that Chelsea was said to have had."

He takes a strand of her hair between his fingers, as if they were back in his bed in the San Juans. "And they won't. Because there aren't any."

"Good." She wraps her fingers around his bicep. "I told Ethan how distraught you were when you came to the ER."

He leans forward and kisses her. Sloane wants to gag when his tongue enters her mouth. Instead, she wraps her hands behind his head and pulls him closer.

"I should go," she says, when he finally tears her lips from his.

"In case Ethan's waiting for me when I get home. I don't want him getting suspicious. He already thinks you may have another phone. You should get a new, unregistered number for us to contact each other."

"He's not going to trace me to that number I've been using."

"You don't know Ethan. I just want to be safe. There's too much at stake now."

"Okay." Brody tucks a strand of her hair behind her ear. "Next time, let's meet somewhere more private." He opens the rear door, and a cold chill fills the car. "Oh, and Sloane? Don't worry about me keeping our affair to myself. You're all I've got left. And I'm not going anywhere."

The door shuts, and she watches Brody put his hands in his pockets as he strides across the gas station parking lot. While she'd known men like Brody Carr existed, she'd never been so close to such a monster before now.

She locks her doors and leans her head against the headrest after he disappears around the side of the building. Maybe she was too quick to judge Crystal for cutting men out of their lives so often.

Her boyfriends likely weren't psychopaths like Brody Carr, but they probably weren't saints either.

Sloane closes her eyes, and for a second, wonders what her mother would do.

If Brody keeps quiet about their affair, everything should be fine. Unless the FBI gets involved. Or Ethan finds a way to charge him with murder. Then, there would be nothing to keep Brody from confessing their affair and casting blame on her.

She glances in the direction she last saw Brody before she throws her car into reverse. When the time comes, cutting ties with him is not going to be easy.

If Brody could so easily kill his wife, and seemingly get away with it, what might he do to Sloane when he finds out she's staying with Ethan?

Chapter 33

E than fills his mug with his fourth cup of coffee in the homicide unit's small breakroom. That morning, he found Jonah poring over the security footage from Carr's mansion when he got to work. As Ethan slung his coat over his chair, he braced himself for his partner to tell him Sloane had been to the app founder's house. Ethan prepared to feign ignorance—and shock—over his wife's relationship with their murder suspect.

Instead, Jonah was riled up: Carr had turned the cameras off on several occasions, almost always in the evenings. As soon as his partner refocused on his laptop screen, Ethan found the link to the footage and scrolled through the dates. He sank against the back of his chair when he saw that one of the gaps in the footage was the night of Sloane's award gala.

But he was only partially relieved. Carr going to such lengths to keep his affair with Sloane a secret didn't mean she was innocent. Only that Carr was good at covering his tracks.

When he had arrived home last night and saw the damage to Sloane's car, he rushed inside, both surprised and relieved to find her reading in bed with a glass of wine, looking unscathed from the accident.

He stopped in their bedroom doorway. "Are you okay? What happened to your car?"

"I'm fine." Sloane set down her novel. "A rock flew up and hit my windshield on I-5. I jerked the wheel when it happened and hit the concrete barrier on the side of the road." She shrugged. "I'm fine though. It looks worse than it was." She lifted her book, flipping to the place she'd left off as Ethan stared at her.

She reclined against a pillow. How could she be so calm and collected after ramming into a barrier on the freeway and mangling the side of her precious Porsche? She's lucky no one hit her. Or that she wasn't hurt. Ethan's eye drifted to her book as she lifted her wineglass to her lips. He recognized the novel he bought her last Christmas that had been left untouched on her nightstand ever since.

His eyebrows knitted together. "It looks *a lot* worse than that. What about your windshield?"

She turned toward him. "Don't worry, I've already called it in to our insurance."

The insurance was the least of Ethan's concern. He pictures Carr behind the wheel of his Maserati, ramming into Sloane's Porsche, trying to run her off the road. Ethan stirs vanilla creamer into his coffee, thinking of the three luxury sports cars he'd seen in Carr's garage yesterday. There wasn't a scratch on them. He shakes his head, forcing the scene from his mind. Imagining Carr attacking Sloane in an act of road rage was doing nothing to further the investigation into Chelsea's death.

"Hey." Jonah pokes his head through the breakroom doorway. "I just got off the phone with Carr's attorney. Carr's agreed to speak with us again, but at his attorney's office in Bellevue. I want to ask who the woman was in the San Juans so we can interview her. You want to come?"

Ethan clenches his jaw as he imagines being in the same room again with the guy. And the look on Carr's face when they ask who he was with last weekend.

"No, I think I'll stay here. I need to check in with TESU and see where they're at with recovering those images."

On his way back to his desk, Ethan pulls out his phone to call TESU and sees he has two new emails. The first is from a local crime reporter asking for an update. The next is from Taryn, the data recovery technician who's been working to retrieve the deleted photos. His pulse quickens seeing the subject line: *Recovered Images*.

He opens the email. *Hey Ethan, I was able to recover three deleted images from the cloud storage on Chelsea Carr's phone. They were deleted on October 22, but I can't tell you an exact time.*

The day Chelsea died. Ethan clicks on the first attachment and sucks in a breath when the image loads. It's Carr with his arm around a teenage girl wearing a crop top and jean shorts. Ethan flexes his jaw, looking at Carr's glossy-eyed smile, his hand around the young girl's bare midriff. *Creep.* She can't be more than fifteen or sixteen. *A kid.*

Ethan clicks to the next photo and leans against the wall. A different young girl sits on Brody's lap on the back of the yacht. In this photo, the girl's face is blurred out. Her arm is around Brody's neck, who looks unaware of the photo being taken. She's wearing only a tiny bikini and unbuttoned cutoff shorts.

The third image is of Carr sitting in the same deck chair with a different young girl on his lap. She's looking away from the camera, giving no view of her face. In the background, Ethan recognizes the notorious Mason Hachette, looking on with a drink in hand.

Ethan closes out of the email. After opening his recent call log, he lifts his phone to his ear. Jonah answers on the second ring.

"What's up?"

"TESU recovered three photos from Chelsea's phone. They're damaging, that's for sure. I'll forward them to you."

"Great."

Ethan grabs his coat as he hurries out of the homicide unit. "I'll meet you at Carr's attorney's office. Don't talk to him until I get there. I want to see the look on his face when we tell him what we've got on him."

Chapter 34

"My client doesn't have long." Carr's tanned attorney extends a hand toward his client.

Carr sits beside his legal counsel in a leather chair on the opposite side of the over-sized desk from Jonah and Ethan.

The attorney straightens his pink silk tie. "He's finalizing a major business acquisition today, which has been needlessly interrupted by your search of his home. But he insists on going out of his way to be helpful."

Jonah forces a smile. "How sweet."

The attorney purses his lips. Carr smirks. Ethan can't wait to wipe that cocky grin off the murdering, cheating asshole's face.

"I'll get straight to the point," Jonah says. "So we don't waste your precious time. Where did you spend this last weekend?"

"At my home on San Juan Island."

"Alone?"

Carr's smirk returns. "No."

"Who were you with?"

"A friend."

"Your assistant said you went to your San Juan Island home last weekend with a woman. Could you give us her name?"

Ethan shifts in his seat.

Carr keeps his eyes on Jonah. "I don't see what that has do with anything."

"We'd like to talk with her, if possible."

Carr's eyes dart to his attorney's, who leans his elbows onto his desk. "My client is willing to help you in determining Chelsea's death was a tragic accident so she can rest in peace. He's grieving the loss of his wife after a heroic attempt to save her. Please don't try our patience."

Jonah leans back in his seat. "Is there a reason you won't tell us who she is? Maybe her *age*?"

"That's enough!" Carr's attorney straightens. "Unless you have something relevant to ask my client, this meeting is over."

Carr crosses his leg. Ethan shoots Jonah a sideways glance before pulling out his phone. He pulls up the first image recovered from TESU and sets his phone atop the desk. He watches the smug look on Carr's face fade as he slides the phone toward him.

"Our technical electronic support unit was able to recover some deleted images from your wife's phone. It appears they are of you, on Mason Hachette's yacht, in the very close company of some very young girls." Ethan studies Carr's hardened expression as he stares at the image.

His attorney slides the phone back toward Ethan. "These photos prove nothing. If you just came here to harass my client, then we're done here. I can't believe this is where our tax dollars go."

Ethan locks eyes with Brody, ignoring the lawyer. "I would hate for these images to fall into the wrong hands. Imagine what your wife thought when she saw these."

The attorney pushes back his chair. "Okay, Detect—"

Ethan speaks over him. "I know what *my* wife would think if she saw these."

Carr's eye twitches.

Ethan scoots to the edge of his seat, not taking his eyes from Carr's. "One look and she'd be gone forever. Repulsed beyond repair."

Brody narrows his gaze. "You don't always know someone as well as you'd like to think. Especially the ones we're closest to." He cocks his head, the sides of his mouth hinting at a smile.

He's enjoying this, Ethan thinks. *And that has to stop.* "All it takes is something like this for a woman to decide who she *does* and *doesn't* want. Even after a nice weekend."

Brody smirks, shaking his head. Jonah and Carr's attorney exchange a look of confusion. Jonah clears his throat before casting Ethan a warning glance.

Ethan rests his elbows on the table, locks his fingers together. "You can bet that with all she's heard, she's already made up her mind about you. With or without those photos."

The attorney waves his hand in the air. "All right, we're done here."

Ethan stands from his chair, keeping his eyes trained on Carr. "The next guy she's with should thank you. You've made him look like a saint."

The attorney looks at Jonah. "Get him out of here."

Jonah grabs Ethan's arm. Ethan pulls out of his reach.

He presses his palms onto the ridiculously large desk as Carr's smug grin morphs into a frown. "A very *screwable* saint."

"Get out!" the attorney shouts as Jonah gives another tug on Ethan's arm.

"Let's go," Jonah barks in his ear.

Ethan turns, shaking out of his partner's hold as he follows him out of the office.

"What was that?" Jonah asks once they're inside the elevator. "It seemed...personal."

Ethan presses the button for the underground parking garage. "I just don't like that guy."

Jonah studies him as they descend the thirty floors to the parking garage. "Okay. You don't want to tell me? Fine," he finally says.

The elevator doors open. Jonah turns after stepping into the parking garage. "The caretaker of Carr's San Juan Island home called on my way here. He said that Carr requested to be alone on the property last weekend, so he didn't see who Carr was with. There are three security cameras outside the home, so I'm going to see if we can get a warrant for the footage from last weekend."

Ethan follows after him, trying to think of a reason to keep his partner from requesting the warrant. He could insist on being the one to check the footage, but if he lies about the contents and is found out, he'll be looking at prison time.

Jonah turns. "What if he told this woman about his plan to murder his wife? We'll never know if we don't ask her. Who knows, maybe she even helped him plot it."

Ethan stops.

"I know," Jonah adds. "I just hope he wasn't preying on some teenager up there."

"That seems like something that happens down in Los Angeles, Jonah. Not the San Juans."

Jonah turns around. "Maybe. Maybe not. You coming back to homicide now?"

"Actually, I wanted to interview the firefighters who responded to Carr's 911 call. See if they noticed anything unusual about his behavior."

Jonah stops after unlocking his Ford. "I'll join you."

"The medic's report said they were dispatched from Fire Station 29."

"Meet you there."

Ethan pulls out his phone after getting behind the wheel. He attaches the three recovered photos from Chelsea's phone in an email to the FBI agent he spoke to earlier that week. After sending the email, he opens the message from the local crime reporter.

Hey Ethan, Got any updates for me about your investigation into Chelsea Carr's death?

Ethan hits *Reply* and then *Attach File*. His finger hovers over the last image sent by TESU, with the girl on Carr's lap, facing away from the camera. He might never be able to charge Carr with murder, but leaking a photo like this would go a long way in ruining his life.

Chapter 35

Sloane looks at the clock on her microwave before pulling a mug out of the cupboard. Being at home, alone with her thoughts, is worse than being at work. Even though all day long she walks past the room where Chelsea died, she can still lose herself in a trauma or full code throughout the day. Here, the minutes crawl at an agonizingly slow pace. She drops a tea bag into her mug as her kettle heats on the stove.

Ethan was already gone when she awoke this morning. He didn't seem to buy her story last night about what happened to her car. She wonders if she should've come up with something better. She couldn't tell him the truth, but she also can't afford for him to think she's lying to him.

She thought reading the novel Ethan gifted her in bed would convince him she was fine. He knew she never read when she was stressed. But maybe it would've been more convincing to have appeared rattled from the accident.

She called him earlier, but he has yet to call her back. Aside from Brody telling her they searched his house yesterday, she has no idea what's going on in the investigation. She needs to make sure Ethan is on her side. She checks her phone for the umpteenth time that afternoon, making sure it's not on silent.

He's avoiding her. And she's worried it's not because of the affair.

She expected Ethan to almost enjoy the fact that she needed him, when she came to him about Brody. Even though what she'd done had to be gut-wrenching for him. She's never needed him like he wanted her to. Now, she hoped it would play in her favor.

But it doesn't seem to be working out that way.

She turns toward the late afternoon sun pouring in through the window above her kitchen sink. She checked the news all morning—another downside of being at home—before finally giving it a rest. There were no reports of what the search of Brody's home yielded, and she wonders what Ethan might have found. Despite Brody's confidence that he has nothing to hide.

Remembering his strong body against hers in the cabin of his boat causes a ripple of revulsion through her core. How could she possibly have enjoyed being with such a creep?

Brody texted her prepaid phone that morning with his new number and had kept the message brief. Too brief. The point of the secret communication was for him to alert her about the investigation—to Brody's mind, so she could help him stay one step ahead of Ethan and the rest of Seattle Homicide. *Now nothing.* She called his new number a few hours ago, but it went to an automated voicemail. And Brody hasn't returned her call.

Her kettle whistles, drowning out her thoughts. She flicks off the stove and pours steaming water onto her tea bag at the bottom of her mug. Sloane watches the transformation and takes a breath. She has to convince Ethan what they have is still worth fighting for. Before it's too late.

After squeezing what's left in her honey container into her tea, she goes to toss the tea-bag wrapper into the kitchen garbage. Seeing it is past overflowing, she grabs the bag and carries it to the garage. The concrete is cold against her bare feet as she glances at her dented Porsche and recalls the day Ethan told her with tears in his eyes that he had slept with his homicide partner. How he—

A clang of metal clamoring against the concrete causes Sloane to whip around. The trash bag slips from her grip as Brody jumps out from behind the shelving against the wall.

Chapter 36

L aughter erupts from the room at the end of the hallway as
Ethan and Jonah follow the firefighter captain through Seattle
Fire Station 29. *Maybe I* should've *leaked the photos,* Ethan thinks.
Or at least given a damning statement against Carr to the media. But
he couldn't let his personal vendetta against Carr allow him to do
something to jeopardize their case, or the safety of any of the girls in
the photos.

Jonah turns to Ethan. "My brother's a firefighter. He only works
like nine shifts a month. Sometimes I think I chose the wrong career
path."

"Yeah, maybe." Ethan nods, feeling a twist in his gut at the cascade
of events that will occur once Jonah discovers Sloane is the woman
on Carr's security footage.

Jonah has already set up a meeting with a judge first thing in the
morning to get the warrant approved for the security cameras at
Carr's San Juan Island home. Ethan could warn Sloane. Have her ask
Brody to get rid of it. But the thought of her contacting him again,
asking him to destroy evidence, makes him sick. He could tell Sloane
to come forward, which would look better than being found out, if
Jonah gets the warrant approved. But before he does either, he needs
to know the truth of her involvement in Chelsea's death.

They come to a large rec room where three leather recliners face a flatscreen TV playing Thursday night football, where the Seahawks are playing the Cowboys on the road. A member of Seattle Fire fills each one. Two more are watching the game from a couch against the wall.

"Yes!" One of them raises her hands in the air as the Cowboys miss a field goal.

"No!" Another emergency responder exclaims, digging his hand into the opened bag of Doritos on his lap. "He's on my fantasy team."

Jackson, the captain who met Ethan and Jonah at the door, reaches for the remote and mutes the TV.

One of the firefighters turns in her seat. "*What* are you doing?"

"These detectives from Seattle Homicide have a few questions about our 911 call with Chelsea Carr," Jackson says.

The three firefighters turn their attention away from the game and sit upright in their recliners.

Jackson motions toward the two guys sitting on the couch. "Hunter and Landon were the two medics who worked on Chelsea. But all six of us responded."

"You guys want to have a seat?" Jackson points to a worn-in couch against the opposite wall to the two medics.

"Sure." Jonah sits.

Ethan sinks into the cushion beside him.

The female firefighter turns serious. "That was a really sad call. So tragic."

"Yeah," Ethan agrees. "As you've probably heard, we're investigating her death."

"A photo of Brody Carr with a young girl just came up on my news feed." The female firefighter lifts a phone from her lap.

Ethan and Jonah exchange a look.

"We haven't released any photos to the public," Jonah says.

The firefighter sets down her phone and looks between the detectives. "Well, someone did."

Ethan wonders if the leak came from the FBI office. More likely, it was the person who anonymously sent Chelsea the photo in the first place. Now he's really glad he didn't send the pictures.

He suddenly worries what Carr's reaction will be to the leaked photo. He has no doubt Carr will blame him for doing it, especially after their last encounter. *Would he retaliate against Sloane? Is she safe from him?*

Ethan turns to the medics, shaking the last thoughts from his mind. "We read your medical report from her resuscitation, but were wondering if you could reiterate her husband's account of what happened when he found her in the water?"

Hunter speaks first. "He was pretty panicked when we got there. In shock, it seemed. He'd been giving her mouth-to-mouth after calling 911. She still had a pulse, but barely, when we arrived. By the time we got her intubated, we lost it."

"There wasn't much time to talk," Landon adds. "We loaded her into the ambulance soon after losing her heart rate, wanting to get her to the hospital as soon as possible. The survival rate, you know, for an out-of-hospital cardiac arrest is less than ten percent."

"He did say that he found her unresponsive, tangled in bull kelp, which was what he'd already told the 911 operator," Hunter says.

Jonah glances at the now-tied football game on the TV. "No witnesses have come forward about what happened in the water. Was there anyone there who saw what happened?"

The two medics shake their heads.

"It was just us and the two patrol officers," the captain says. "It had been raining on and off. The beach—and that park—were empty."

Ethan leans forward, resting his elbows on his knees. "And did you notice anything unusual about Brody Carr's behavior?"

"No," Landon says, his coworkers shaking their heads in agreement.

"He seemed distraught." Hunter looks pensive, as if replaying the scene in her head. "Rightfully distraught."

"What about at the hospital?"

Ethan shifts uncomfortably in his seat at his partner's question.

The emergency responders exchange glances.

"He didn't get there until after we left," Landon says.

"Oh, okay. And there was nothing to make you think her drowning was anything other than an accident?" Jonah asks.

A siren blares from the room's built-in speakers, causing the three seated firefighters to jump from their recliners.

"Oh, man. We're gonna miss the end of the game." Hunter looks back at the TV before following the firefighters and other medic out of the room.

Jackson turns to Ethan and Jonah before heading toward the door. "The only thing a little strange—and this is when we got her to the hospital—is that the doctor bit a nurse's head off when he asked about giving Narcan. Which is weird, because I've seen her in action quite a few times, and she's normally really nice."

Sloane. Ethan feels like he's just swallowed a box of nails.

Jackson hurries after his cohorts.

Ethan frowns, his head spinning from what the fire captain said. Carr made a point to bring up Chelsea's current opiate addiction when they first interviewed him. But there's no evidence to support his claim. Did Sloane know Chelsea would have drugs in her system? Did she ensure Chelsea wouldn't be revived?

Jackson turns when he reaches the door to the garage. "You guys can let yourselves out, right? No guarantees when we'll be back."

Ethan gives him a wave. "Right, will do."

Jackson disappears into the adjacent garage.

Jonah elbows Ethan. "Dude, you think he was talking about your wife? Doesn't she work at Bayside?" Jonah smirks.

The wail from the firetruck and ambulance's sirens compiles with the piercing alarm inside the station. Ethan covers his ears with his hands.

"I'm just kidding, man," Jonah yells, making no move to get up from the couch. "It wasn't her, right?"

Ethan made sure he was the one who received the medical report from Bayside. And he never shared with his partner that it was Sloane who treated Chelsea at the hospital. While his old partner might have started making the connection between Sloane and Brody, Jonah seems oblivious. But how's it going to look that Ethan omitted the little fact of Sloane being the one who pronounced Chelsea dead?

"Um." Ethan turns his attention to the TV, pretending to focus on the game. "With our long hours, I haven't seen her in a few days. I'd have to look back at the report from Bayside."

He feels Jonah staring at him out the corner of his eye. "Or...you could just ask her."

"Yeah." Ethan gets up from the couch and heads toward the main entrance. "How do you think Carr's going to react to that photo getting leaked?"

Realizing Jonah isn't beside him, he turns.

Jonah moves toward a recliner as the alarm stops, moments before the sirens fade away. "Well, he's not going to be happy, that's for sure. He's likely already committed murder to keep that photo from surfacing. And he's probably going to think you leaked it, after the way you laid into him at his attorney's office."

Jonah unmutes the TV before plopping into the leather chair and reaching his hand inside the bag of Doritos that was left behind.

Ethan's mouth drops open. "What are you doing?"

"There's only three seconds left." Jonah motions toward the flatscreen where Seattle's kicker is lining up for a field goal. "Come on, have a seat."

But Ethan doesn't move. He follows Jonah's fixed gaze to the game, zeroing in on the kicker as he prepares to make a game-winning field goal. Ethan recognizes the pressure encased within the athlete's eyes as he looks between the goal posts. Every single play of the game now comes down to him.

Feels familiar.

Jonah tilts the bag of Doritos toward him after crunching one inside his mouth. "Chip?"

Chapter 37

Brody lunges toward Sloane with his hands outstretched.

For a moment, she hardly recognizes him. Gone is the lovesick man who hid in her backseat last night, and the grief-stricken husband who cried over his wife's death at the hospital. There is a deranged look in his eyes, open so wide they bulge from his face. His brown waves stick out in all directions from his head.

She screams. He covers her mouth with his palm and presses his other hand against the back of her head as she tries to get away from him.

He lowers his face toward hers, gritting his teeth. "*Shhh!*"

She screams again, but the noise is muffled against his hand.

"Why would you lie to me, Sloane? Ethan *knows* about us. He's coming at me hard."

Still trapped in Brody's grip, Sloane tries to shake her head, *no*.

"Oh, yes, Sloane, he does. With a personal axe to grind on top of it. Your *husband* leaked a photo of me with a half-naked woman sitting on my lap. And, and...because her face is blurred out, now everyone is assuming she's underage. Do you even understand what that means for me? To my company?"

She frantically scans the tools hanging on the wall for something she can use as a weapon. Her eyes settle on a hammer. The only problem is she'll have to get past Brody to reach it.

He follows her gaze. "Don't even think about it."

Her phone is in the kitchen. She uses both hands to pry his palm away from her face and shakes out of his hold. She pivots when he reaches for her and runs toward the door to the house. His arms wrap around her torso before she gets past him. He lifts her into the air. She flails her arms and legs before Brody slams her back against the metal shelving.

"*Ahh!*" She cries out in pain, as a bin filled with Christmas ornaments falls from the shelf.

"Stop!" he yells, when she opens her mouth to scream again. Spittle escapes his mouth and lands on her cheek.

"I don't know what you're talking about!"

"Ethan went to extra lengths to recover those photos from Chelsea's phone. Why would he do that, Sloane?"

"Brody, calm—"

"Calm? Okay, Sloane. Listen to this *calm* story. Thanks to your husband, one of those pictures has just gone viral. And the FBI is refusing to comment on questions from the media. And you know why? Because they just opened an official investigation into me based on new evidence of my involvement with Hachette, that's why." He encircles his hands around her upper arms as his voice grows several decibels louder. "The One's stocks have tanked, and I lost the acquisition of Crush. The world thinks I'm a pedophile *and* a murderer!"

His red eyes look crazed. His mouth stays open, exposing his teeth as he shakes her by the shoulders. For the first time, she is truly terrified of him.

"I'm not stupid, Sloane." He tightens his grip around her arms, keeping her pinned against the shelf. "I won't be hung out to dry while you hide behind your detective husband. What have you told him?"

"Nothing!" She pushes against the metal shelf digging into her spine and shoves his collarbone with both hands.

He doesn't budge. Doesn't even blink.

"Then how does Ethan know about us?"

"I don't know!" She tries unsuccessfully to wriggle out of his hold. "You're hurting me!"

He brings his face closer to hers. For a moment, she thinks he's going to kiss her, but he stops when his face is an inch from hers.

"I'm on your side." She looks him dead in the eyes. "I haven't told Ethan anything."

"Good. Because we're a team, Sloane. And you don't want to be my enemy. I'm a powerful man. If Ethan arrests me, you can be damn sure you'll become the prime suspect in Chelsea's murder. Imagine the world hearing my side of the story. How it was your idea. That you talked me into killing her. Made sure you'd be the doctor who treated her at the emergency room. Ensured that her failed resuscitation ended with you pronouncing her *dead*. There will be a toxicology report, along with the autopsy. You know that, right?"

Her heart thumps inside her chest, but she refuses to gratify him with an answer.

"I crushed up three oxycodone and mixed them into Chelsea's coffee before we went diving." His lips twist into a smile. "You didn't give her Narcan, did you?"

She glares back at him. "There was no reason to."

He lifts his eyebrows. "Especially if you didn't want her to be revived."

She narrows her eyes.

"Even if you aren't convicted, you think Ethan will stay by your side? That Bayside Hospital will still employ you? That any hospital would? Think about it."

She clenches her jaw. "Get out of my house."

"You've got to do better, Sloane." His voice takes on a fierce tone she hasn't heard before. "You don't get to play innocent while my life goes up in flames. Get Ethan off my back. Do your part."

"How am I supposed to do that? I have no control over his homicide investigation! You're the one who's gotten yourself into this mess—not me."

He frowns. "Maybe Ethan needs to have an accident." A look of satisfaction comes over his face as Brody takes a step back. "Oh, come on. You're a doctor. I'm sure you can think of something."

Sloane feels a lump form in the back of her throat. "You're sick."

"My attorneys are getting their hands on Chelsea's medical report from the ER. Soon, I'll have the names of everyone who was in that room with you when she died. Right now, it's your word against mine. But it won't be for long."

Sloane ignores the sting in her back as she steps away from the shelf. "I tried to save her!"

Brody's hand clamps around her throat before she can react. "Save your lies for your husband!"

He thrusts the back of her head against a storage bin. Sloane runs her hand across the storage shelving. Brody's hands stay at her throat as Sloane closes her grip around the cold steel handle of a wrench. Sloane sucks in a deep breath. Brody takes a step back, keeping his eyes trained on hers.

She lifts a hand to her throat, keeping a tight hold on the wrench in her other hand. She narrows her eyes at him while her breathing returns to normal.

"You don't want to play me, Sloane. I always win." He turns and strides past her Porsche toward the side door of the garage that leads to her yard.

She is still standing against the shelving when he opens it and whirls around.

"Don't forget what I said about Ethan."

A wave of fear ripples through her when he smiles.

After Brody disappears out the door, Sloane sinks to the cold concrete floor and pulls her knees to her chest. She rubs her neck. *Maybe it's time I go to the police and come forward about the affair.* How else would she get Brody to leave her alone?

But if what Brody said about the oxycodone is true, and he accuses her of withholding the Narcan intentionally? There would be no way to disprove it. His word against hers.

Sloane brings her hand to her face. *How did everything get so spun out of control?* Out of all the men she could've picked to right the capsizing ship of her marriage, why did she have to pick a murdering psychopath?

Lifting her gaze to her Porsche, she raises the wrench above her head. "*Ahhh!*" She screams, hurling the steel wrench into the hood of her car.

The tool hits her car with a metallic clang before clamoring to the concrete floor. She stares at the dent, reminded of the devastating news photos of Crystal's Firebird after she drove it into a telephone pole. She'd always been so quick to judge her mother's choices, assuming it was her lack of trying that caused things not to work out.

Sloane's chest heaves with every breath. Is this how Crystal felt before she hit that pole? Helpless? Out of control? Scared? If the news of her affair gets out, Sloane would look to the rest of the world like just another jealous girlfriend driven to murder. She swipes away a tear with the back of her hand when her doorbell chime fills the garage.

Chapter 38

"Man, nothing like watching the Hawks win in overtime," Jonah says as they leave the fire station. He turns to Ethan when he reaches his car. "Hey, I'm heading to interview the patrol officer who gave Carr a ride to the hospital. I know we read her report, but I want to see if she remembers anything off about him. You want to come?"

"Actually, I've got an errand to run. But I'm headed back to homicide afterward."

Jonah waits for Ethan to elaborate, but he doesn't.

"All right." Jonah opens his driver's door. "I'll see you there. I've gotta work on that warrant for Carr's security footage."

After getting into his car, Ethan pulls out his phone and dials Bayside Hospital's ER. He's put on hold for a few minutes before a woman comes over the line.

"Bayside emergency and trauma center, how can I help you?"

"Hi, this is Ethan Marks. I'm Sloane's—Dr. Marks's husband. Is Dr. Evelyn Chang working today?"

"Yes, she is."

"Could I speak with her?"

"Let me check if she's with a patient. Can I put you on hold?"

"Yeah, thanks."

Classical music comes through the phone speaker as Ethan merges onto the West Seattle Bridge.

"This is Evelyn." She speaks fast, with the impatience of an ER doctor with other things to do than be on the phone.

"Hi, Evelyn. It's Ethan. Ethan Marks."

"Sloane isn't here today."

"I know. I wanted to talk to you. I was wondering if you could clarify some things for me from Chelsea Carr's medical report."

A pause. "Why don't you ask Sloane?"

Because I don't trust her. "I know you're busy, but I'd really appreciate it if you could give me your opinion on some things. I could bring you a coffee?"

She breathes into the phone. "Okay, fine. I can meet you at The Evergreen Café beside the hospital in half an hour. But I can't stay long. And I'll take a decaf latte."

"You got it. And thank you."

Chapter 39

Her doorbell rings again, longer this time. Sloane pushes herself to her feet and takes a deep breath before going inside. The doorbell chimes a third time as she moves through the house. She stops, wondering if Brody has come back.

She tries to make out the figure through the frosted glass of her front door, wishing she had taken the time to install the doorbell video camera on their front porch. It's been collecting dust in the entryway cabinet practically all year.

She can tell it's not Brody from the lean silhouette. It's a woman. Her hand still trembles from Brody's attack when Sloane unlocks the door and swings it open.

"Oh." Ethan's mother, Kay, retracts her hand from the doorbell. "Hello, dear. I was starting to think you weren't expecting me."

Sloane is at a loss for words as Kay brushes past her into the house, trailing her Louis Vuitton suitcase behind her.

"Thanks for having me." she adds.

Her mother-in-law's Chanel perfume catches in Sloane's throat, still aching from Brody's grip. Sloane scans the empty street in front of her house for Brody.

"I Ubered from downtown," Kay says, following Sloane's gaze.

Sloane closes the door, her mind still focused on Brody as she tries to make sense of her mother-in-law's impromptu visit from California. Being the founding partner of the biggest legal firm in the Bay Area makes her a busy woman. In the nearly ten years she's been married to Ethan, her mother-in-law had never visited Seattle. Sloane hasn't seen her since her late husband's funeral last March.

"Is everything okay?" Kay glances toward the direction of the garage. "I thought I heard a scream."

"Oh." Sloane clears her throat. "Yeah. I just got home from...um...yoga."

Kay raises her eyebrows.

"And someone marked up the hood of my car while I was in class." Sloane motions toward the garage. "I was just assessing the damage. And it's pretty bad."

Her mother-in-law puts a hand over her heart. "That's terrible. I'm so sorry, dear." She shakes her head. "Crime seems to be on the rise everywhere these days. I hate going anywhere in San Francisco without secure parking. I'm just glad you're okay."

Sloane forces a smile. "Thank you."

What on earth is she doing here? And why did it have to be now?

Kay's heels clack against the hardwood floor as Sloane follows her into the living room. Her platinum-blonde bob is teased a good inch at the roots, adding to her already tall stature. Kay stands a good head taller than Sloane's own mother, and Sloane wonders what Kay would think of Crystal if she were still alive.

Kay is a well-kept woman, sparing no cost in her appearance. Crystal bleached her hair from a box, still sporting a perm in 1998. Even without money, her mother's beauty would outshine everyone else in the room. There was a fire in her eyes that Sloane has never seen in anyone else.

"My meeting with the new corporate client finished early, so I thought we could drive together to the restaurant. But maybe we should get an Uber after what happened to your car. Unless Ethan can drive us?"

Sloane fights to shake the image of Brody's gritted teeth and wild eyes when his hand clenched around her throat. *What restaurant?* Sloane racks her brain but is sure she's never heard anything from Ethan—or Kay—about this visit. Or dinner plans.

Kay furrows her brows. "Did Ethan not tell you? I thought I'd stay the night rather than fly back right away. Take you two to dinner. He said you'd both be free. I spoke to him about it a week ago."

Sloane feels a stab of resentment at her mother-in-law's words. Ethan can make definite plans a week in advance with his mother? *Why can't he ever do that for me?*

Kay eyes Sloane's attire before continuing. "I made us a reservation at Vito's for eight."

Sloane glances at her leggings and faded t-shirt embellished with the rock band Heart. "I forgot," she lies. "I'm so sorry. Things have been a little hectic at the hospital lately." She forges an apologetic smile. "It skipped my mind it was tonight."

"I completely understand. So..." Kay looks around the empty living room. "Will Ethan be meeting us there?"

Sloane doubts that Ethan ever told his mother about his affair. And now he's conveniently left it to her to pretend everything is great between them.

"I'm not sure. I'll send him a text and see what time he'll be done with work."

Swallowing the distaste in her mouth at Ethan's unmentioned plans with his mother, Sloane moves into the kitchen to get her phone.

"Great," Kay says. "I'll just put my things in the guest room."

Her words barely register as Sloane grabs her phone off the kitchen island and types a text to Ethan. *Did you forget to tell me you made plans with your mother and invited her to stay? Nice that she can count on you to put her before your work.*

She bites her lip before pressing *Send*, thinking of Brody's threats. She can't afford to drive Ethan farther away. She deletes the text and starts over. *Your mother's here. Will you be meeting us for dinner?*

After she hits *Send*, she hears Kay's heels clicking against the floor of the upstairs hallway. She swears and bounds up the stairs. When she reaches the top, Kay is retreating away from the guest room, pulling her suitcase back toward the staircase.

"Sorry," Sloane says. "Ethan and I have been working opposite schedules lately, so he's been sleeping in the guest room so we won't disturb each other. It won't take me long to make up the bed."

Kay swipes a hand in front of her face. "No need. I'll get a hotel."

"No really—"

She puts a hand on Sloane's shoulder. "It's fine, dear."

Her all-too-knowing eyes remind Sloane of Ethan's. She's too smart a woman to buy Sloane's story. She and Ethan have had crazy work schedules their entire relationship, but it's never kept them from sleeping in the same bed.

"I don't want to get in the middle of..." Kay glances toward the guest room. "Whatever you two have going right now."

She pats Sloane's shoulder before starting down the stairs. "Why don't we head to Vito's early? I could use a drink before dinner."

Me too.

Kay turns when Sloane starts to follow her down the steps, smoothing her leather trench coat. "Didn't you want to change first?"

Sloane looks down at her outfit. "Oh, right."

Chapter 40

E than gives Evelyn a wave when he spots her enter the coffee shop next door to Bayside Hospital. The place isn't busy at this time of evening, and he snagged them a table on the opposite wall from the coffee house's few other patrons.

"Thanks for meeting me."

Evelyn's long hair is pulled back, and she wears a jacket over her blue scrubs. She takes a seat across from him, looking less than thrilled as she wraps her hand around her latte. "It's decaf, right?"

He nods.

She takes a sip. "I can't stay long. We're really busy."

It's obvious she doesn't like him. Sloane doesn't have friends outside of her work, so naturally she told Evelyn, her closest coworker, about Ethan's affair. It's easy to see from Evelyn's judging eyes that she's deduced him to be the *asshole cheating husband*.

"I'll make it quick." He slides Chelsea's medical report from the ER across the small table. "Is there anything here that looks unusual to you?"

She furrows her brows after glancing at the printed report. "Why don't you ask Sloane?"

"I did. But being my wife, there's a conflict of interest. A defense attorney would shoot that down. So, I need another opinion. From someone I'm not married to."

She shrugs. "All right, fine."

Ethan takes a drink from his black coffee as he waits for her to look over all the pages. She pushes the short stack of papers in his direction after she scans the last page.

"Nothing unusual. The resuscitation went according to procedure. I wouldn't have done anything differently." Ethan leans his elbow onto the table. "You were working that day, weren't you?"

She nods.

"Did you notice anything unusual?"

"What do you mean?"

"Well, Sloane was in the middle of Chelsea's resuscitation, so she might not have noticed her husband's behavior as well as someone who was able to more objectively observe. Were you?"

"No. I was on break when Chelsea Carr was brought in. She was supposed to be my patient, but Sloane took over for me. I feel bad now since—"

"Wait. What do you mean Sloane took over for you?"

She sits up straight. "Why are you asking?"

"I'm just covering my bases. Standard procedure. I don't know how everything works in the ER."

"Okay. Well, I'm pregnant and wasn't feeling very good."

"Oh, congratulations. Sloane didn't tell me that."

Evelyn gives him a slight nod. "Thank you. That's why Sloane let me go on break even though she was supposed to go first, since her shift started before mine. Anyway, she seemed shaken by Chelsea's death afterward—some patients hit you harder than others." She stops to take a sip of coffee. "I'm sure she's talked to you about it, already. It can be hard having a young, healthy woman brought in like that and not being able to save her. I feel bad, since I should've been the one leading the code."

Ethan works to keep his expression neutral. *Was Sloane shaken because she realized her lover had killed his wife? Or because she helped him?* "Shaken? How?"

Evelyn brings her latte to her lips again but pauses before taking a drink. She narrows her eyes. "In the normal way a doctor is shaken when you can't save a young, healthy patient. Do you really think you're in a spot to be asking these questions of your wife? Treating her like a *suspect?*"

"No, that's not—"

She stands from her seat. "I could trust Sloane with my life—anyone could. You, on the other hand? I wouldn't turn my back on for a second." She shoves her chair toward the table with a screech. She lifts her cup in the air before she turns. "Thanks for the coffee."

"Asshole." Ethan hears her mutter under her breath as she walks away.

Ethan considers what she said as Evelyn moves past the window outside in the direction of the hospital. *Sloane took over for me.*

He pulls his phone from his pocket and sees he has a new text from Sloane, sent a half hour ago. *Speak of the devil.* He stands after reading her text, remembering his mother is in town. He pushes in his chair and heads for the door.

Chapter 41

"I know it's not my place, but is everything okay between you and Ethan?"

A live jazz band plays in the corner of the busy Italian restaurant where Sloane sits across the table from Ethan's mother. She takes a drink from her second glass of Cabernet before answering. Reservations at the restaurant along Post Alley at Pike Place Market were hard to come by, having to be made at least several days in advance, especially for a Friday night. But Kay managed to get them a window table at the second-story restaurant. The Ferris wheel glows a bright magenta from the pier at the waterfront.

Sloane clears her throat. "Yes. Great."

Kay would never understand what had transpired between her and Ethan. Her in-laws had a seemingly perfect marriage. Having met in law school at Yale, they were bonded by sharing the same career path. And their mutual love for their child. They were partners in every aspect of their lives.

Kay assesses her, and Sloane shifts uncomfortably in her seat. She can see where Ethan gets his interrogation skills from. It was as if the woman could see right through her.

"Mother."

Sloane looks up to see Ethan. A charismatic smile forms on his face when Kay meets his gaze. Sloane can't remember the last time he looked at her like that as she watches him kiss his mom on the cheek. His smile dissolves when he briefly locks eyes with Sloane, before taking the seat beside her.

"Hi," is all he says before turning back to his mom. "Sorry I'm late."

Sloane feels heat rise to her cheeks as Kay looks on. *Is he really apologizing for being five minutes late?*

"How's your work?" Kay asks pleasantly.

His work. Sloane reaches for her wine, finding herself wishing for normal married people problems. *Not* that the man she cheated with was the center of Ethan's homicide investigation. And soon, she could be too. If she isn't already.

"Good. I just came from an interview pertaining to my new case. At Bayside Hospital, so it wasn't far away. Funnily enough, I was interviewing a colleague of Sloane's."

Sloane chokes on her wine. Ethan and Kay turn in her direction as she brings a hand to her chest.

"Something bothering you, Sloane?"

He turns and fixes his eyes on hers, and she avoids his knowing stare. From his cold expression, she worries that Brody has already accused her. She envisions her ex-lover in their garage. He's become completely unhinged. Or maybe he always was.

Maybe she should tell Ethan about Brody's impromptu visit in their garage. But not in front of his legal queen mother. *Who was he interviewing? Logan?* But she's too afraid to ask. Instead, she shakes her head.

"No. Just went down the wrong pipe."

Kay turns to her son. "Such a shame what happened to Sloane's car."

"What? Oh, right." Ethan shoots Sloane a wary glance. "I'm just glad she wasn't hurt. Or hit by another car after she slammed into that concrete barrier."

"No, this was *today*." Kay motions toward Sloane with a manicured hand. "She said it looks as though someone took a hammer to her car while she was parked at her yoga studio earlier." Kay purses her lips while shaking her head. "No city is safe these days."

Ethan cocks his head toward his wife while answering his mother. "I wasn't aware Sloane did yoga. Ever."

"Ethan, you're missing the point." Kay raises her voice a decibel. "It must've been horrible for her to come out and find that damage to her hood. Especially after what happened to her car the other day. She told me all about it. And it's such a lovely car."

"*Hmm.*" Ethan keeps his eyes on Sloane.

Kay lifts the bottle from the middle of the table and gestures toward Ethan's glass. "Wine?"

"No, thanks. Actually, I can't stay long. I have to get back to work. I've just learned some valuable information that I need to follow up on."

Sloane looks out the window, refusing to meet his gaze. Her heart hammers against her chest hard enough she's afraid Ethan can hear it.

Kay returns the bottle to the table. "What's all this I've been hearing in the news about Chelsea Carr?"

Sloane tries to keep her eyes from widening as they dart toward her mother-in-law.

"So awful about her husband's involvement with Hachette and those underage girls." Kay lifts her wine. "Is that your case?"

Ethan nods. "Sure is."

"Sloane's had a busy week too," he adds. "Haven't you?"

Sloane turns toward him. He frowns. She feels a rise of panic as he casts her a knowing stare, while his mother looks on from the other side of the table.

Is he referring to her weekend with Brody or being the doctor who pronounced Chelsea dead? Or both?

"I suppose that's the life of an emergency room doctor," Kay says.

"Yes. Sloane went to college with him. Did she tell you?"

Kay's eyebrows lift in fascination. "Oh, really? With Brody Carr?"

Sloane glances at Ethan, whose attention is refocused on her. "Just one class. I didn't know him."

"Strangely, Sloane was the doctor who pronounced Chelsea dead."

Sloane feels like a brick has landed in her stomach. She gapes at Ethan. There's a hateful look in his eyes, and she feels a wave of fear travel through her.

"Well, I suppose that makes sense that your work would overlap occasionally," Kay says. If she picks up on Ethan's accusatory tone, she doesn't show it. "Isn't Bayside the biggest trauma center in the region?"

Sloane exhales. "It is."

A waitress approaches their table, and Ethan scoots back his chair. "I have to go. I'm sorry, Mom, that I don't have more time." He stands and moves around the table to plant another peck on his mother's cheek.

She smiles, patting his hand on her shoulder. "No problem. I understand."

"I'll call you tomorrow and see if I have time to meet before you head back to the airport." He shifts his attention to Sloane. "I don't know what time I'll be home."

Without waiting for her response, he turns and maneuvers through the crowded restaurant for the door.

"What can I get for you two lovely ladies this evening?" their waitress asks.

Sloane moves her spinach linguine around on her plate, too consumed with dread over Ethan's earlier comments—and what they meant—to eat.

Kay eyes Sloane's full plate from across the table and sets down her fork, using her napkin in a most immaculate fashion. Sloane's mind flashes back to the rickety dining room table at home with her mom.

"You know, Roger and I went through some hard times in our marriage."

Sloane is tempted to smile, imagining what *hard times* she is referring to. Roger leaving his towel on the bathroom floor? A disagreement over which was the better private school to send their son to? Or where to go on vacation?

"Roger cheated."

Sloane looks up from her pasta. Ethan always painted a picture of his parents having a happy union. To Sloane, they seemed to be one of the most genuinely happy couples that she had encountered. At Roger's funeral, Kay seemed devastated.

"With a young associate," she continues. "It was right after I had Ethan."

"So how did you...?"

"Move on?" Her eyes narrow, and she leans back in her chair. "I let the affair play out, knowing he'd get bored with her after a while. And he did. I saw them having an argument in Roger's office not long after Christmas. We'd just returned from a family vacation in Aspen, where I'd made a point of reminding him of all that he would lose if we were to divorce. Soon after, she quit. Roger never knew that I knew."

This surprises Sloane. Not just Roger's infidelity, but that a woman as strong as Kay could look past it. "But didn't it bother you? I mean, how could you just look the other way?"

Kay smiles. "It did. But I wasn't going to let some young associate take away everything I had worked for. Everything that was *mine*. It took me a while to get over it, but once I did, I was glad that I hadn't let my emotions get in the way of having the life *and family* that I deserved." She looks pensively out the window. "Some might say I was weak, but it took strength not to let my emotions take over and confront him about the affair. I didn't want Roger to stay with me out of guilt. He could've left me if he wanted, but because I was patient, he chose me. And once I forgave him, we really were happy together again." She returns her gaze to Sloane's. "Even today, most men still expect women to act a certain way. They put us in a box, underestimating us. We react emotionally, not rationally. Incapable of making a clear plan and following through on it. All that stuff. It's easier than you think to sway a man's decisions, while making him believe he's still in control." She lifts her wine glass by the stem. "Despite his shortcomings or perhaps momentary lapses in judgement, Ethan loves you. Just like his father loved me. You're the one he picked to share his life with. Maybe you need to decide what it is *you* really want. And how far you're willing to go to get it."

Sloane takes a large bite of her pasta, considering Kay's advice. Her mother-in-law is right. Something needs to be done. While there's still a chance for her and Ethan. Before Brody ruins her life.

Within minutes, Sloane's plate is empty. She wipes her mouth with her napkin, seeing Kay is not even half-finished with her meal.

"That was delicious." She lifts her glass and takes a long drink from her wine.

Right now, there is only one person driving her and Ethan apart. And it won't be long before his threats became a reality. She's got to get to him first.

Chapter 42

Logan marches toward Sloane when she steps out of a treatment room. When he spotted her that morning, Logan rolled his eyes. "You needed more than one day off, Dr. Marks," he said, as he filled a mug with breakroom coffee before the start of their shift.

After she dropped Kay at her hotel last night, the hospital called. Sloane figured she might as well keep busy while she decides how to deal with Brody. She got a text from Evelyn before going to bed saying she wanted to talk to her today, but so far, there's been no time to chat.

"The potassium on Grant Hopkins, the patient in treatment room four, just came back as two point two," Logan says when he gets closer. "He's Evelyn's patient, but she's tied up with the patient who was just brought in with septic shock."

Sloane drapes her stethoscope around her neck. "Start a potassium chloride infusion at thirty mEq's an hour. I'll let Evelyn know when she's done."

Sloane moves toward a desk beside the wall and logs onto the computer. She pulls up one of her patient's charts, pretending to read while she takes a moment to think.

If what Brody said yesterday was true, Chelsea's toxicology would come back positive for oxycodone. Would Ethan's colleagues find out she shouted at Logan not to give Narcan? She's guessing Ethan already knows this. Why else would he be acting so sure of her guilt?

"I've got the patient in treatment room seven prepped for stitches."

Sloane turns to see Rachel standing beside her.

"Thanks. I'll be right there."

Biting her lip, she logs off the computer. There is no easy solution.

Logan meets her eyes after stepping out of a nearby treatment room, rubbing hand sanitizer between his hands. "I just got that potassium infusion started. When do you want the next potassium level?"

"Um." She tries to blink away her thoughts. "Thirty minutes."

He crosses the hall and leans against the desk beside Sloane. "Evelyn also ordered insulin for that patient, Grant Hopkins. Should I hold off until we get that next potassium level?"

"Yes, hold off." They both know the insulin would lower the patient's potassium level even farther. "What was the blood sugar?"

"Two hundred and two."

Sloane stands from her chair. "Yes, don't give it for now. I'll go let Evelyn know before I stitch up room seven. What room is she in?"

Logan steps around the desk and logs on to the computer beside her.

"Treatment room ten," he says after a few clicks.

He points to the patient's name. "It's Samuel Lucas."

The name sounds familiar.

"He was brought in a couple of weeks ago after a heroin overdose," Logan adds.

Sloane remembers now. "Oh, right." He was a known member of a fast growing—and increasingly violent—White Center gang.

A call light dings outside one of the treatment rooms.

Logan logs off the computer. "He was brought back in septic shock—with a bunch of fresh track marks on his arms."

He heads in the direction of the blinking call light.

"Hey, Logan?"

He turns.

"Did Ethan talk to you yesterday?"

Logan's brows knit together. "Your husband?"

Sloane nods.

"No. Why?"

Sloane shrugs. "Oh, it's nothing. I'll go let Evelyn know about that potassium level."

Sloane moves down the hallway as Logan answers the call light. *If it wasn't Logan that Ethan interviewed yesterday, who was it?*

Evelyn would've told her if it had been her. Plus, she wasn't a part of Chelsea's resuscitation. When she gets to treatment room ten, it's empty aside from a nurse clearing supplies off a procedure cart.

Sloane stops inside the doorway. "I'm looking for Dr. Chang."

The nurse tosses the used supplies into the trash before turning her way. "Her patient just got taken to the ICU. I think she went to the bathroom." She pulls off her gloves and hurries out of the room.

Sloane spots a Carhart coat draped over a chair in the corner. It was probably removed by the medics or ER team. She lifts it off the chair to take it back to the nurse's station when something in the inner pocket clunks against the chair's metal armrest. She reaches inside the coat and feels the smooth, hard barrel of a pistol.

"I think the patient's coat got left in here."

Sloane jumps from the nurse's voice behind her. She grips the gun's handle and slides it out of the coat's pocket and into the front pocket of her scrubs. She turns around, forcing a smile as she holds the coat out toward the nurse. "This must be it."

"Thanks." The nurse hurriedly reaches for the garment before disappearing down the hall.

Sloane presses a hand gently against the weapon in her scrub top when she steps out into the hall, afraid to let it bounce around for fear it might go off. Not to mention that someone might recognize the outline of a pistol in her pocket.

Evelyn steps around the corner of the corridor at the same time as Sloane. "Hey."

"Oh!" Sloane puts her other hand to her chest.

Evelyn laughs. "Sorry, didn't mean to startle you. I heard you were looking for me."

Calm down. Sloane nods while taking a slow breath.

"What'd you need?"

"Um..." All Sloane can think about is the pistol in her pocket. From the weight of it, she guesses it's loaded.

Evelyn looks at her expectantly, the smile fading from her face the longer it takes Sloane to respond.

"Oh. I had Logan start a potassium infusion for your patient in room four, Grant Hopkins, for a potassium of two point two. I also had him hold off on the insulin until after he gets another potassium level. Just wanted to let you know."

"Okay, thanks." Evelyn crosses her arms, glancing behind her before taking a step toward Sloane. "Ethan came to see me yesterday. Asking about Chelsea Carr." She's nearly whispering. "Is everything okay between you two now?"

Evelyn hadn't seen Sloane shout at Logan not to give Narcan. *So why had Ethan seemed so sure of my guilt after talking to her?*

Sloane forges a smile. "Yeah, things are great. Why?"

"Well, he kept saying that his questions were standard procedure. That he needed a second review of Chelsea Carr's medical records, since yours would be a conflict of interest, being you're his wife. But..." She tilts her head to the side. "He seemed to get fixated on you letting me go on break before Chelsea Carr was brought in. So, I explained to him it was because I'm pregnant."

Sloane nods, masking the angst building in her chest from Evelyn's revelation.

Evelyn shrugs. "The conversation just seemed...a little weird, I guess."

"*Hmm.*" Sloane presses her lips together. "Knowing Ethan, I think he was just being thorough."

Evelyn uncrosses her arms as she appears to weigh Sloane's words.

"We're happier than ever now," Sloane adds.

"Good. I'm glad to hear it." Evelyn's eyes drop to Sloane's hand on her front pocket. Frozen still, Sloane resists the urge to follow her gaze. *Just be cool. She can't see it.*

The sides of Evelyn's mouth lift into a smile when she looks up. "You *are* pregnant, aren't you?"

Sloane swallows, feeling herself nod. "Yes. Yes, I am."

Evelyn's eyes widen with joy.

"It's still really early, so don't say anything to any—"

"Of course, I won't!" Evelyn pulls Sloane into a hug before she can stop her.

Sloane steps back, afraid Evelyn could feel the outline of the gun behind Sloane's hand. "*Shh!*" She looks around, but they're alone in the corridor.

"Sorry," Evelyn whispers, lifting her shoulders. "Congratulations!"

"Thanks." Sloane steps to the side, giving Evelyn a wide enough berth that she doesn't go in for another hug as Sloane moves past. "I'm actually not feeling well. Can you stitch up the patient in treatment room seven while I run to the locker room?"

"You got it." Evelyn winks. "And your secret's safe with me."

Sloane hurries down the hall, keeping a hand against the gun. *What the hell am I doing?*

As she strides down the hallway, her eyes rest on treatment room six, the room where Chelsea died. In that moment, she knows the answer to her own question: She's doing what has to be done.

Chapter 43

"D r. Marks!"

Sloane turns.

Logan is coming toward her with swift steps. "Your husband's here."

Sloane presses her hand against the gun in her pocket. She hasn't talked to Ethan since his brief appearance at the restaurant last night.

"He's in the waiting room. You want me to tell him to come back?"

"That's okay. I'll go out there.

She walks down the hall toward the waiting room and tries to look relaxed while keeping a firm hand against her front pocket.

Sloane steps into the waiting room and spots Ethan maneuvering through the crowded space in her direction.

"Hey." He holds out a coffee from the Evergreen Café. "I got you a latte."

Behind him, a red-faced toddler cries hysterically atop his mother's lap as she tries unsuccessfully to console him. Sitting next to them, an elderly man cradles his head in his hands.

"Thanks." Her fingers brush his when she takes the cup. After how he acted at the restaurant, his visit has to be more than to bring her coffee.

"I didn't hear you come home last night."

His eyes are red from lack of sleep. "It was after one. You were asleep."

She takes a sip, aware of the hard gun barrel pressing against her abdomen. Fortunately, Ethan hasn't moved his pointed stare from her face.

"I need to talk you," he says. "Alone."

Sloane glances around the overfilled waiting area. "I'm not sure where we'll find that here."

"How about outside?"

"Okay." She follows him through the congested space.

When they near the outside doors, Sloane has to practically step over a homeless man she recognizes from his frequent ER visits who is lying across the waiting room floor.

"Make it stop!" the man screams, when he spots Sloane.

Sitting in a chair behind the screaming man is a middle-aged man with a broken nose and bloodied piece of gauze affixed to his forehead. He leans his head against the window beside him as the homeless man's screams subside.

The cold air is a refreshing reprieve when they step out the double doors. They move side by side down the sidewalk. Ethan stops once they're several feet from the entrance.

"Jonah got a warrant approved for the security footage on Brody Carr's San Juan Island home."

"What does that have to do with Chelsea's death?"

Ethan crosses his arms. "Jonah knows Carr was with a woman there last weekend after talking with Carr's assistant, and he thinks this *mystery woman* might be able to shed some light on Carr's role in his wife's death."

Sloane stares at the lid of her coffee, thinking of the cascade of events once Jonah learns she was sleeping with Brody Carr the weekend before pronouncing his wife dead. And then how she failed to come forward about it. "Isn't there something you could do—"

"No!" Ethan's eyes widen. "There's nothing I can do, Sloane!" He glances in the direction of an ambulance pulling into the parking lot, the wail of its siren drowning out her name. He drops his hands to his sides before bringing them to his hips. "I tried to help you, but this is out of my hands." He points his finger toward her, something he's never done in their entire relationship. "You got yourself into this. Now it's up to you to get yourself out."

"How am I supposed to do that?" she yells over the siren, aware of the weight of the pistol in her front pocket.

The ambulance pulls to a stop in front of the ER's double doors, the sound of the siren replaced by the vehicle's doors opening. Ethan shoots another glance in its direction, but Sloane doesn't turn around. It's Evelyn's turn for a new patient, not hers.

Ethan's wary eyes return to hers. "We should have the footage by tonight. So, if you hurry, you can ask your old pal to delete it. Maybe you'll get lucky and he already has. But I doubt he's gone to such lengths to protect you. And if not, you should be ready for some very hard questions. Questions I hope you have a good answer for. Because I'll be honest, Sloane." Ethan leans toward her.

"What was his last BP?" she hears Logan ask one of the medics as they roll the patient inside.

"Seventy over forty."

Ethan's red eyes remain fixed on hers. "The odds of your *innocence* in all this are becoming...real thin. Even for someone who wanted to give you the benefit of the doubt."

Sloane reaches for his hand, but he pulls away. His jaw is set, and she doesn't like the way he's looking at her. Does he really think, after a decade of marriage, that she's guilty of premeditated murder? She thinks of Kay at dinner after Ethan left.

"I'm scared of Brody. I should've told you before, but he's been stalking me. He was waiting inside my car the other night after work—"

"What!" Ethan takes a step back.

The ambulance driver turns in their direction.

Sloane steps forward. "I thought I could get him to leave me alone, but he's become totally unhinged. Since this whole thing with his wife."

"You should've told me."

"I know." Her hospital phone rings. She sighs and pulls it out of her pocket. It's the nurses' desk. She holds up a finger to Ethan to indicate she'll just be a minute. "Dr. Marks."

Ethan is already walking away.

"Hi, Dr. Marks. It's Rachel—"

"I'll have to call you back."

After hanging up, she starts to jog after him, but stops suddenly when she feels the pistol jiggle inside her pocket. "Ethan, wait!"

He wears a pained expression on his face when he turns. "I have to get back."

"Is there any way you can delay Jonah getting that video footage? Or at least watching it?" There has to be something he could do.

He shakes his head. "This is all the help I can give you."

"Brody's dangerous, Ethan."

"If you see him again, you call me. Don't go anywhere near him. No more secrets, Sloane."

She nods. "Got it."

He walks away without another word.

The waiting room hasn't gotten any less crowded in the few minutes she was outside. The homeless man is still lying on the floor between two rows of chairs, but his screams for help have morphed into indiscernible utterings under his breath. Sloane heads straight for the locker room, keenly aware of the pistol in her scrub top.

"Dr. Marks?"

Rachel steps out from the nurses' desk when Sloane hurries past.

"Just a minute." Sloane holds up one finger, quickening her steps.

Rachel purses her lips.

"I'll be right back."

When she reaches her locker, she glances around to make sure she's alone before she swiftly slides the gun into her purse.

She can't trust Brody to delete his security footage from the San Juans. Not after his threats in their garage. Even if she could convince him to do it, how would it look if they were caught conspiring to cover up the evidence of their affair? It would only confirm their mutual guilt. And if they weren't caught, the footage in Brody's hands would only give him more ammo to use against her. He's never going to let her be free of this.

Which leaves her no choice but to free herself.

Chapter 44

S loane looks up from the couch when Ethan walks into the living room. "Thanks for coming home."

He sinks into one of the costly designer armchairs Sloane ordered at the same time as their barstools. "You're welcome."

The security company who serviced Carr's San Juan Island home told Jonah they'd send the requested footage over first thing tomorrow morning. Jonah had already gone home when Ethan got Sloane's text saying they needed to talk.

The gas fireplace flickers in the dimly lit room. Sloane is still wearing her scrubs and refills her wine glass from the opened bottle on the coffee table. "Wine?"

"No, thanks."

Ethan watches her lift her glass to her lips, preparing himself for his wife to confess her role in murdering Chelsea. She returns her glass to the coffee table before meeting his eyes.

"Brody snuck into our garage yesterday and attacked me. Before your mother came."

"*What?*" He stands from the uncomfortable chair, scanning Sloane's face and arms for a sign of injury from Carr's attack.

He balls his hands into fists, imagining that sadistic prick inside his garage, coming at his wife.

"He threatened to make it look like I conspired with him to kill Chelsea if I didn't help him." She scoots toward him.

"Why didn't you tell me?"

Because your mother showed up, then you came at me guns blazing at dinner. "I thought I had it handled."

Ethan paces in front of the fireplace. Thinking about that murdering bastard breaking into his house makes his skin crawl.

"Brody's crazy, Ethan. Delusional. Dangerous. He's never going to let me be free of this. I thought about what you said earlier, and I want to come forward about our affair."

Ethan stops.

"We'll say you didn't know," Sloane continues. "That I just told you tonight, and you advised me to make a statement in the morning."

Ethan runs his hand down the back of his head.

"I can't see any other way out." Sloane glances at her purse lying atop the coffee table beside the wine. "And believe me, I've thought of everything. This is the only way to keep Brody from having a hold on me. I know it'll make me a suspect, at least for a while, but there's no way they can prove I helped Brody kill his wife. Because I didn't."

He starts pacing again, not sure of what to say. If Jonah finds out Ethan knew about Sloane's affair, he could lose his job. His entire career. What had been his purpose in life.

"Will you go with me? Help me?"

He stares at the floor, remembering what Evelyn told him when they met for coffee. And the firefighter's account of Sloane shouting at the nurse not to give Narcan.

"Ethan!" Sloane stands from the couch. "Will you? And can you *please* stand still?"

He spins toward her. "No! No, I can't. I talked to Evelyn. I know you told her to go on break so you could take over as Chelsea's doctor. And that you uncharacteristically shouted at a nurse when they asked you to give Narcan."

"Because I knew Brody drowned her!"

Ethan steps forward, putting his hands on his hips. "How?"

She sighs, glancing at the wine on the coffee table. "I went freediving with him in the San Juans, and the same thing happened to me."

Ethan frowns. "What do you mean?"

"I got tangled in bull kelp. Brody had to cut me free. He—he saved me."

Ethan's stomach twists into a knot.

Sloane meets his gaze with pleading eyes. "That's how I knew it wasn't an accident. And why I didn't give Narcan. Because I was certain he drowned her."

"What in the hell made you think that Carr wanted his wife dead? So he could be with you?

"There were things said in the San Juans that would lead me to believe that, yes."

"Awesome, just awesome. What happened yesterday when he jumped you in the garage? Did he hurt you?"

"He was panicked. The news had just hit about the picture of the girl. And...he told me that he crushed some oxycodone into his wife's coffee before they went diving. Probably to ensure she wouldn't put up much of a fight."

"Oh, wow. Her toxicology report will show it." He thinks of Carr bringing up his wife's opiate addiction when they first interviewed him. "He wants to pin this on you."

Sloane moves around the coffee table toward him. "I know. But no one can prove I knew about it, which I didn't. Even if I *had* given Narcan, it's hard to say whether it would've made a difference at that point."

Unable to look at her, Ethan turns. He stares at the flickering flames.

"I wish I didn't have to come forward, but there's no other way out of this. Believe me, I've thought of everything. Best case scenario, my career will be tainted forever."

Ethan whirls around, shocked at her words. "Are you *seriously* talking about your career right now? *That's* what you're worried about?" He scoffs.

She steps toward him.

"You're unbelievable." He backs away. "But while we're on the subject, *your* career won't be the only one that's jeopardized."

"So, you'll help me?" Her pleading eyes search his. "Go with me in the morning?"

He studies the woman he once thought he knew. How the hell did they get here?

He exhales. "Yes. I'll go with you."

Her face relaxes. "Thank you."

He strides out of the room, heading for the stairs.

"What are you doing?"

"I'm going to take a shower." He needs to think. About what Sloane has told him and what he'll say to Jonah tomorrow. He's going to have to do his fair share of acting, but Jonah will likely believe Ethan was in the dark about Sloane's affair.

Chapter 45

Sloane waits until she hears Ethan's footsteps upstairs to pull her prepaid phone from her purse. She rereads Brody's earlier response to her text. Before leaving the hospital, she sent him a message saying she'd decided to come forward to Ethan and his homicide partner about their affair. *You're not going to threaten me anymore.* Despite how they'd left things yesterday in the garage, he replied within seconds. *You don't want to do that. Let's talk about this.*

A few minutes later he sent another. *Sloane, talk to me! Don't do this.*

Then another. *Where are you? I'm driving into the city. Let's meet.*

She nearly smiles at his arrogance. Did he really think, after coming at her like that, she was going to listen to him? She types her response. *I'm in the last place you saw me. My garage. Remember that, Brody? Jumping in the car to head to the police station.*

Brody immediately responds. *No! Stay there. Just hear me out. I'm coming right now.*

Upstairs, the bathroom door closes as Sloane sends another message to Brody. *I don't know if that's a good idea.*

Seconds later, her phone lights up with another reply. *Already in the neighborhood. I'll be there in five.*

Her heart races as she slides the phone back inside her purse. While she was counting on this, she's suddenly filled with nervous adrenaline at what she's about to do.

She hears the shower turn on above her. She pulls the pistol out of her purse, grateful Ethan has showed her how to use a firearm. It was never her thing, but he took her shooting a few times when they were dating. Having already checked the magazine, which is nearly full, she pulls back on the slide to chamber a round.

Seeing the lights from Brody's Maserati pull in front of the house through her front window, Sloane flicks off the safety and moves toward the front door. She hears his car door shut. She listens for the water still running upstairs, then opens the door before Brody has a chance to knock.

"Why are you doing this?" He steps inside without waiting for an invitation. "Because of yesterday? Look, I'm sorry. It was a hell of a day."

Sloane moves aside, keeping the gun tucked slightly behind her as she softly closes the door. He turns around after reaching her living room. He looks tired, but also calm. The crazed look from yesterday is gone from his eyes. His fitted black jacket reminds her of what he wore when she bumped into him at the Kirkland Market.

"You'll only be implicating yourself by confessing our affair. You know that, right? When I say I told you all about Chelsea's drug addiction, you'll look like the jealous mistress who ensured Chelsea was taken out of the picture. It would probably make things better for me, but I'm trying to help you."

Sloane wants to laugh that he thinks he's somehow in charge. All because he killed his own wife.

He puts his hands on his hips. "Kind of makes you think, doesn't it?"

Sloane steps toward him without a word. She stops a few feet away, keeping the gun tucked behind her back.

"Well?" Brody's eyes narrow into slits. If he's aware of the water running upstairs, he doesn't show it.

"I've already made up my mind. I'm going to tell them how I know you drowned her. Because it almost happened to me. How you snuck into my car, broke into our garage, attacked me, and told me about the oxycodone. How you planned to use it against me if I came forward."

His nose curls into a snarl. "Oh, no you're not. Did you tell Ethan how you wanted him dead? How you were the one to bring it up after screwing me in the bathtub?"

Sloane doesn't respond. Instead, she slowly moves her finger off the gun barrel and onto the trigger.

Brody steps toward her. "And how you adamantly refused to give Narcan?"

She ignores the tension that builds between her shoulders.

"That's right. My private investigator talked to one of the first responders." He smiles. "You *shouted* at the nurse not to give it."

His smile fades. "What's that noise?" He points at the ceiling.

He gapes at her as the water upstairs turns off. His eyes double in size.

"Is Ethan *home?*"

Sloane swings her arm forward and aims the stolen pistol at Brody's chest. He throws his palms in the air. "Whoa! Sloane, calm down!"

"Trust me, I'm calm."

Brody's eyes dart toward the ceiling. "Ethan!"

Sloane fires a round into the fireplace. The glass shatters as her ears ring from the blast. Brody lunges for the gun.

"Ethan!" she screeches.

She lets the gun fall to the floor as Ethan's bare footsteps pound down the upstairs hallway. Brody jumps for the gun. He comes up looking terrified and angry all at once.

He aims the pistol at her. "Stay. Back."

Sloane steps toward him, seeing her husband fly down the stairs, dripping wet, clutching a towel around his waist, his gun drawn with the other.

"Be careful, Ethan! He has a gun!"

Brody looks back at Sloane, his brows knit together in horrified confusion. "What are you—"

"He tried to kill me!"

Brody's terror-filled pupils lock with Sloane's before his eyes dart toward Ethan, who stands huffing at the foot of the stairs.

"Drop the weapon!" Ethan yells. "Now! Drop the gun!"

Brody swings the weapon at Ethan. "She's the one—"

Sloane screams over Brody's voice.

A blast fills the room. Brody's head recoils from the impact of the bullet to his forehead. Sloane brings her hands to her face as she watches him recoil and collapse to the floor. Ethan rushes over, and Sloane pulls the weapon out of Brody's limp hand seconds before Ethan can. She looks away before she steps over Brody. His eyes seem fixed on hers as the life drains from them.

Sloane turns to Ethan beside her and allows him to take the pistol from her grip. He stands holding a gun in each hand, staring at the blood draining from Brody's lifeless form.

"Call 911." Sloane bends down and feels Brody's neck for a pulse, realizing her words came out calmer than she meant them to. "My phone's in the kitchen. The passcode is our anniversary. Tell them we're starting CPR. It will look better if we do."

"I'll use mine. It's upstairs. I have to get dressed anyway." Ethan rushes out of the room, seemingly in shock over killing Brody in their living room. Sloane hurriedly pats down Brody's pockets as soon as Ethan is out of sight. She feels two phones, one in his jeans' pocket and the other in his jacket.

Upstairs, she hears Ethan already talking to the 911 operator. She uses Brody's finger to unlock the phone from Brody's jacket and taps the messages icon on the home screen. Seeing her texts from earlier, she slips the phone into her scrubs pocket, leaving his other phone untouched. It strikes her that this was fortunate. She would have had to explain her fingerprints if she touched the other one.

She hears Ethan's voice coming down the stairs. "Yes, my wife is doing compressions." A pause. "No, there was no pulse."

Seconds later, Ethan appears in the living room dressed in a t-shirt and joggers, holding his phone at his side.

"I thought you were going to start CPR?"

On her knees beside Brody, Sloane sinks back onto her heels. "I said it would *look better* if we do. It's not like you gave him a chance to survive. Shooting him in the head like that."

Ethan puts his hands on his head. Sloane notices his hair is starting to gray at the temples. He looks at Brody's body lying beside her, before his eyes rest on hers.

"What happened? Why did you let him in?"

"He knocked on the door, and I couldn't tell who it was. I asked, you know, *who's there?*, before opening the door, and he said he was your partner, Jonah. As soon as I unlocked the door, he came rushing in with a gun." She motions toward the pistol now sitting on the coffee table.

Ethan's eyes trail hers.

"He started waving it around, saying crazy things," she continues. "Just like he did in the garage yesterday. Demanding to know if I'd told you about our affair and why I hadn't done something to end the investigation. As if I could *do* anything. I told him to leave, immediately, and then he took a wild shot at me." She waves her hand in the air for emphasis. "That's when I yelled for you."

Outside, the wail of sirens grows closer as the emergency responders turn onto their street.

Ethan looks toward the flames flickering through the shattered glass panel of their fireplace.

Sloane follows his gaze. "He said he'd kill me for not helping him look innocent."

The sirens fill their quiet street, no doubt drawing the attention of all their neighbors, before coming to a stop in front of their house. Red lights flicker outside their front window as Sloane presses the heel of her hand on Brody's sternum.

"We'll stick to what we were going to tell your partner tomorrow. That you just found out about my affair with Brody tonight."

Ethan nods as he backs toward the door to let them in.

The doorbell rings as Sloane starts compressions. She stares into Brody's lifeless hazel eyes and the growing puddle of blood mixed with a splatter of brain matter beneath his head.

Ethan leads two medics, one pushing a stretcher, into their living room. They are followed by four EMT firefighters.

"My wife's an ER doctor," she hears Ethan say.

She continues to compress Brody's chest when the two medics reach her side.

"He was shot once in the head," Sloane tells them. "He immediately collapsed and went pulseless. I've been doing CPR for five minutes."

After allowing the emergency responders to take over the resuscitation efforts, Sloane moves away from Brody's side.

She can feel Ethan's eyes on hers as she watches the medics attempt to revive Brody. She turns toward her husband of nearly a decade, and a look passes between them. She searches his blue eyes, unsure if he believes her story. She offers him a faint smile, but he doesn't smile back.

But she is sure there won't be anyone alive to dispute it. The front door opens, and a patrol officer steps inside. Ethan leaves Sloane's side to go speak to her.

Sloane looks back at the medics who are attempting to intubate Brody, knowing their efforts are futile.

"I can help if you need me to," Sloane says.

They continue compressions as Sloane recalls Kay's advice at the Italian restaurant. She lost sight of her goal after everything Brody had done, but Kay's words had reground her in what she'd set out to do in the first place. After all, she always knew how far she was willing to go to get what she wanted.

As far as it takes.

Chapter 46

Ethan looks up when the door to the small interview room opens, seeing the detective specializing in officer-involved shootings. She's been going back and forth interviewing Ethan and Sloane for the last hour. Jonah had been called to the scene at Ethan's house shortly after the medics arrived, but the investigation had quickly been taken over by two separate entities outside of Seattle Homicide.

Seattle's FIT, force investigation team, is conducting an internal investigation to determine whether Ethan's actions were covered by SPD policy, while King County Major Crimes is taking over the criminal investigation into Brody's death. Shortly after Ethan and Sloane arrived at Park 90/5, a multi-building complex separate from SPD headquarters and precincts, Ethan learned Brody Carr had died at Bayside Hospital. Even though the shooting had occurred at Ethan's home when he was off duty, it was still protocol for the force investigation team to take over the investigation.

The tall redheaded detective takes a seat across from Ethan and the representative from the police guild who sits beside him. The police guild rep sports a suit, but his hair sticking up in all directions at the back of his head is a telltale sign of being summoned from sleep to be present with Ethan. Ethan looks at the FIT detective, feeling strange to be sitting on this side of the interview table.

The detective rests her elbows on the table. "So, to reiterate, tonight was the first time you learned of the affair between your wife and Brody Carr?"

Ethan holds her gaze. "That is correct, yes."

She leans back in her metal chair. "CSI found Carr's prints on your garage door, which matches your wife's statements about him attacking her yesterday." She interlaces her fingers and rests them on the table. "Are you aware how long this affair between your wife and Brody Carr was going on?"

Ethan shrugs. "Sloane said they bumped into each other a little over a month ago, but they only became physical or whatever over the last week or so. But like I said, it was news to me tonight."

She nods. "So, when you came downstairs, a shot had already been fired."

"Yes."

"And you didn't hear Carr come in? Your wife said he rapped on the door a few times before she answered."

Ethan was already thinking about this as he sat alone in the interview room, waiting for the detective to finish interviewing Sloane. If Brody came in like Sloane said, rapping on the door before wildly threatening her and waving around the gun, why hadn't he heard anything until the shot was fired? Would the shower really muffle all that commotion?

Ethan shakes his head. "I was in the shower. I had just dried off and was putting my boxers on, to tell you the truth, when I heard the shot."

"The pistol Carr brought to your home is unregistered, and there's no report of a sale linked to it. It wouldn't have been hard for someone with Carr's means to get his hands on a gun like that. We'll send the pistol to the crime lab and see if it can be linked to any other shootings."

He envisions his wife, so calm and collected as Brody bled out beside her on the floor. Sure, she was no stranger to trauma, but after coming so close to taking a bullet to her face, she wasn't even rattled. And how she so easily put on a show of doing compressions for the first responders, as if she'd been trying desperately to save Carr's life.

What was she afraid would happen if Carr lived? Out of nowhere, their marriage therapist's words pop into his mind. *Think the best of each other, not the worst.* Sloane had been telling the truth about Brody attacking her in their garage. She probably just didn't want to live with the threat of him coming after her again. If that was the case, he can't say he blames her.

The detective stands from her chair. "Thanks for your cooperation, detective. As you know, you'll be on leave until we, and King County Major crimes, conclude our investigations. I'll let you know by email if I have any more questions. You can meet your wife outside in the hall."

She opens the door, waiting for Ethan and the police guild representative to exit first.

Ethan follows the guild rep out of the room. Sloane is leaning against the wall, still wearing her scrubs, which are now stained with blood. Jonah is standing beside her. Her eyes look red from crying, a stark contrast to her cool and collected demeanor after Ethan shot Brody.

He thinks back to the instant before he pulled the trigger. Seeing Brody lift his gun toward Sloane's terrified face. He couldn't lose her. He loves her, despite everything.

She grabs his hand. "Let's go home."

But can he trust her?

Jonah slaps Ethan on the shoulder. "Everything's gonna be okay. I'll drive you two."

Ethan wants to believe his partner's words as Jonah leads the way down the hall toward the exit.

As they move down the quiet hallway Sloane squeezes his hand, and he feels himself squeeze hers back. Maybe this was their chance. To put the past behind them. And start fresh.

Chapter 47
Five Weeks Later

Sloane wakes to the sensation of Ethan's lips on hers. Her eyes flutter open, and she smiles when he pulls away. The early morning sunlight filtering in through their drawn bedroom curtains is enough for Sloane to see he's already dressed for work.

"I'll see you tonight," he says.

She reaches behind his head and draws him toward her for another kiss.

"Bye, detective." She yawns as he pushes himself off their bed, straightening his suit as he heads for the door. "I love you."

He turns. "I love you, too."

Sloane sits up in bed when she hears the garage door open, knowing she won't be able to go back to sleep. She lifts her phone from her nightstand to check the time. She has over four hours before she meets Kay for lunch. She throws back her comforter and pulls on her silk robe lying draped over her chair.

She peeks through the blinds of her bedroom window, glad to see that the news crews that lined her street the first few weeks following Brody's death haven't returned. She watches Ethan's Fusion pull away from their drive before moving away from the window. Sloane envies him being able to return to work, while she remains on administrative leave. Due to SPD's staffing crisis, Ethan returned to work the day after being cleared of any wrongdoing in Brody's death.

After reviewing Chelsea's resuscitation, Bayside's ER medical director sent the case review up the chain to the hospital's Medical Staff Quality Committee for a second opinion from another physician. Which meant the director must have found fault, or at least something in question, with Sloane's resuscitation of Chelsea Carr. She wonders if the hospital is dragging its feet while they wait for Chelsea's toxicology results, even though Sloane knows it shouldn't matter. Ethan has assured her that even if Chelsea's toxicology shows opiates in her system, there is no way to prove Sloane was aware of it. And if Seattle Homicide can't prove it, neither can Bayside.

She flicks on the bathroom light before opening the cabinet beneath her sink, reminding herself there's no need to worry. Bayside's review of Chelsea's resuscitation would be based solely on whether Sloane acted within standards of medical practice. Which she did.

She pulls the pregnancy test from the box and unwraps it before sitting on the toilet. Although there were a *few* hiccups, her plan to use Brody to save her marriage had worked. After taking the gun from the ER, she took the time to wipe down the pistol and every bullet in the magazine so it couldn't be easily traced to the previous owner. And though they had the wrong person, investigators theorized Brody did exactly that.

The bullets came back a ballistic match to bullets used in an armed robbery from 2018. From what the FIT detective told Ethan after she closed the case, she suspected Brody bought it off the street. He knew it would be hard to trace.

Sloane pees on the tip of the pregnancy test and sets it on the back of the toilet while she waits for the results. She stares at the test, willing a plus sign to appear as she simultaneously braces for a single blue line, indicating a negative result. She bites her lip. She's only a few days late.

It took Ethan a while to warm to her after he shot Brody, even though he's been sleeping in their bed ever since that night. She can tell Ethan doesn't fully trust her yet, but he's getting there. The investigation backs up her innocence, and being a detective, he respects that. In time, he'll let go of all his suspicions. But for now, the sex is great.

Her heart sinks when the flat blue line appears after a minute. She lifts the stick, about to toss it in the trash when a faint line appears perpendicular to the horizontal one. Her eyes widen as the line darkens, forming a blue cross.

She stares at the results, afraid if she looks away the second line might disappear. But there is no mistaking the dark blue cross that remains on the stick. She spins around and catches her reflection in the mirror. *I'm going to be a mother.* It is a more daunting thought than she expected. For the first time since she was on her own in life, she feels incredibly ill-prepared. *I don't know how to be a parent.*

But she and Ethan will figure it out together. She can already imagine the look on his face when she tells him. It's what he's wanted for so long. He'll be consumed by it. They'll be parents. A family.

Chapter 48

Jonah glances up from his desk when Ethan walks into their cubicle, but doesn't offer a greeting.

Ethan expected some awkward stares when he returned to work. After all, his wife had an affair with a billionaire app founder, whom Ethan shot dead in their home, and it made international news. But his coworkers hardly look or speak to him at all, if they can avoid it. It is way worse than when news went around the department about him and Rachel. He doubts things will ever be the same. Even with Jonah, who's already re-engrossed in his computer screen.

Seeing the bags beneath his partner's eyes, Ethan feels guilty he didn't get to work earlier, though it's just after seven. In the three weeks he'd been put on administrative leave, Jonah had been handling both of their caseloads.

"What's this?" Ethan points to the case file sitting atop his laptop after draping his coat over the back of his chair.

Jonah lifts his coffee mug toward his mouth. "McKinnon assigned you to an assault case that happened overnight."

"Another one?" While getting the occasional assault case on top of their homicide caseload had become routine in the last couple of years, getting one every day was not.

"I guess Christmas came early." Jonah shrugs, not bothering to look in Ethan's direction.

Ethan reaches for the folder containing the new assault case.

"Hey, Marks."

Ethan turns to the sound of his sergeant's voice.

"We just got another assault, a stabbing in the Fremont area, along Aurora." McKinnon strides into their cubicle with a folder in his outstretched hand, matching the one on Ethan's desk. "Sorry, I had to assign it to you. Adams and Stevenson worked a new homicide all night, and Richards and Suarez just got called to a double shooting."

"That's all right." Ethan takes the folder from McKinnon's hand.

"Thanks." McKinnon pauses before returning to his office. "How are you doing?"

"I'm good. Thanks, Sarge."

"Glad to hear it." McKinnon turns from the cubicle.

His sergeant, at least, is more understanding than most. Ethan opens the case file that had been waiting on his desk that morning first. A photo of a woman with a black eye and a laceration on her left temple is clipped to the first page of the report. Her long, wavy blonde hair reminds him of Chelsea Carr's.

While Chelsea's manner of death remains *undetermined* by the medical examiner, Jonah had at least been able to give her parents some peace of mind in knowing Carr confessed to Sloane that he killed their daughter. His confession alone to Sloane, however, wasn't enough evidence to charge him posthumously with her murder.

As he flips through the case file, his thoughts drift to the image of Sloane, smiling at him in their bed that morning. He wants to trust her again. He'll never forget the terror that ripped through his body when he thought Brody was going to shoot her. But even with the evidence from the investigation backing up her claims, there's still something in it all that doesn't sit right with him. Having watched her so easily lie about their affair and be so quick to fake her resuscitation efforts after he shot Carr gives him a gnawing feeling that he can't shake.

He returns his focus to the assault case when Jonah's desk phone rings.

"Detective Nolan."

Ethan reads the assault victim is thirty-two-old Hannah West, who was attacked on her way to a bus stop last night at eleven p.m. on her way home from work. There were no witnesses, and it was on a poorly lit street, so she didn't get a good look at her attacker. He was wearing a dark hood, had a beard. He came at her from behind, hurling his fist into her face when she turned around, before swinging a blunt object at the side of her head. She collapsed and passed out. An Uber driver called 911 after finding her ten minutes later. Ethan finds that the only upside to the report.

"Okay, thanks," he hears Jonah say before hanging up. "That was Pete." His partner's voice takes on a wary tone. "Chelsea Carr's toxicology just came back."

Ethan spins around. "And?"

"It's positive for oxycodone. It doesn't change her cause of death being drowning. Pete said the amount of opioids in her system wasn't likely enough to cause respiratory depression, although it would depend on her tolerance for the drug. It does explain why she didn't put up much of a fight to free herself. Or fight off her husband, if that's what happened." Jonah taps a pen against his desk. "We will have no way of knowing whether she took them herself or if

Carr somehow slipped them to her." Jonah lifts his gaze to Ethan's. "Which adds to the other things we don't have answers to in this case."

From the look on Jonah's face, it's clear one of the *things* is Sloane's possible involvement in Chelsea's death. After Jonah turns back to his desk, Ethan does the same. He stares at the open case file, thinking back to when the fire captain told him and Jonah about the ER doctor shouting at the nurse who suggested Narcan.

Behind him, Jonah rolls back his chair. "I've got a witness to interview. Call me if you need me."

"Okay." Ethan shuts the case file.

"Oh." Jonah stands from his chair. "Maybe your wife told you already, but I got word Bayside finished their medical review of Chelsea's resuscitation this morning. Found *no* evidence of malpractice in Chelsea's medical care. So, there's that. The hospital thinks they can trust her. " Jonah walks out of the unit without waiting for his partner to respond.

Leaning his elbows on his desk, he presses his hands together and lets his chin rest against the sides of his fingers. Sloane said she had no reason to believe Chelsea had drugs in her system, but after all he's seen of Sloane in the last couple of months, can he really trust that she's telling the truth?

"How did the affair start?" Ethan asked her a few weeks ago after they went to bed. "I mean, you're not on social media, and you said you hardly knew him in college."

"I bumped into him when I was buying your huckleberry ice cream at the Kirkland Market on our anniversary," she said, lying next to him in the darkness. "Actually, he bumped into me. Literally. I think he did it on purpose, after recognizing me. He said my name almost immediately after it happened." Sloane rolled onto her side and rubbed her bare leg against his. "After everything that's happened, I wonder if he'd been stalking me beforehand. Waiting for the right time to approach me." She turned onto her back and let out an audible sigh. "Maybe not. He was just so...obsessed. Nothing would surprise me about him anymore."

He pushes the conversation from his mind and reopens the case file in front of him. The assault victim lives in Shoreline, about a twenty-minute drive north from downtown. He stands from his chair and pulls on his coat. Maybe she would remember more about her attacker today than she did last night, now that the shock of the attack has hopefully subsided some.

After merging onto I-5, Ethan exits onto the floating 520 bridge across Lake Washington, rather than continuing north. They sell the huckleberry ice cream he likes at the Magnolia Market. *Why had Sloane gone all the way to their other store in Kirkland?* Fifteen minutes later, he pulls into the already-full parking lot of the Kirkland Market. *Maybe they were out of huckleberry in Magnolia. It was their anniversary, after all.*

"Can I help you?" a girl who couldn't be older than twenty asks when he approaches one of the checkout counters.

It wasn't even eight o'clock and the store was already packed. He'd been waiting in line for over ten minutes.

"I'm Detective Marks from Seattle Homicide, and I'd like to take a look at your store security footage from October first, if you still have it."

He knows it's likely too late. Most stores only keep their security footage for ninety days, but smaller businesses like the Kirkland Market are more likely to only keep them for thirty.

Her pleasant smile fades. She glances around as if she might be in imminent danger. "Um. Did you say *homicide*?"

"I did. I'm looking for something possibly related to an ongoing investigation," he lies. "Do you know if you still have your security footage from that date?"

She swallows. "Let me just check with my manager." She waves her hand to get the attention of a middle-aged man straightening an aisle end display of organic honey. "Hey, Rick? Could you come here?"

The man walks toward them wearing a matching green apron to his employee behind the counter. The cashier points to Ethan when the manager approaches.

"This man is a detective from Seattle Homicide. Wanting to know how long we keep our security footage."

Beyond them, an elderly woman slows her cart, watching them intently before turning down an aisle.

The manager turns his attention to Ethan, raising his eyebrows. "Oh. We keep ours for ninety days." A grave shadow crosses over his face. "Did something happen here I should be aware of?"

"No. I'm just looking for something that might help in an ongoing investigation. Would I be able to view the footage you have from the evening of October first?"

Ethan holds his breath as the manager seems to think it over. There is no way Ethan can get a warrant if he asks for one.

"Sure." Rick glances at the entrance as several more shoppers enter the store. "But I won't have time to go through the footage until later today, unless you want to go have a look for yourself. We're short-staffed and busier than usual with Thanksgiving coming up."

Ethan thinks of the assault victim from last night. And the second, untouched case file still sitting atop his desk. "Later today is great." He pulls out his card with his email and extends it to the manager.

Normally, Ethan would give the business a link to upload the footage directly to the department's official website for digital evidence collection, where it would get logged and linked to a specific investigation.

"Okay." The manager inspects the card. "Detective Marks. I'll email you a link to view the footage from the night. It might be early evening by the time I send it over."

"Thank you."

"Excuse me?" a tall, dark-haired woman with a toddler on her hip comes to a stop beside Ethan, her exasperated gaze fixed on the manager. "Do you have that organic cranberry sauce made from that farm in Grayland?"

The manager tucks Ethan's card into his apron and nods. "Right this way."

Chapter 49

Sloane takes a seat beside the window overlooking the Seattle waterfront at the same table she shared with Kay just over a month ago. She looks around the busy Italian restaurant as she waits for Ethan's mother. Every table is filled, despite it being eleven thirty a.m. on a weekday.

She spots Kay entering the restaurant. She's wearing oversized designer sunglasses, though it's an overcast November day, and takes them off as she makes toward their table. Sloane stands, unsure of how to greet Ethan's mother. It's the first time she's spoken to her since the news of her billionaire ex-lover getting fatally shot by Ethan in their home made the news.

"Hello, dear." Kay offers a slight smile as she sits down across from Sloane. "You're looking well."

Sloane nearly grins. It must be her pregnancy glow. "Thank you."

Their waitress appears as soon as Kay pulls in her chair to take their drink orders.

"I'll start with a sparkling water," Kay says.

"I'll do the same."

Their waitress steps away. Sloane looks across the table at Kay, trying to gauge her expression. She's not completely surprised Kay wanted to meet after the media frenzy that transpired after Ethan shot Brody in their home. When Kay invited her to lunch, she made it clear she wanted to see her alone.

After their waitress returns, Sloane takes a sip of her water, thinking of the blue cross on her pregnancy test that morning. Kay will be the only grandmother her child will ever know, and for that, Sloane wants to maintain the best relationship possible. Their waitress moves to another table, and Sloane braces herself for Kay to berate her for cheating on Ethan.

Kay lifts her menu. "After all that came out in the news about you and Brody Carr, Ethan told me he cheated on you after his father died."

Sloane brings a hand to her mouth as her water catches in the back of her throat. *Here we go.* She expected to have at least a few moments of false pleasantries before Ethan's mother brought up the subject of who they were sleeping with.

"You know..." Kay's mouth forms a slight frown as she skims the menu. "When we ate here before, I thought maybe Ethan had an affair with Chelsea Carr. The way you two were acting so strangely about Ethan's investigation. But now it makes sense."

"We both made a mistake."

Kay looks up from the menu with intelligent blue eyes the same color as Ethan's. "Ethan made a mistake. Your affair with Brody Carr seems a little more calculated than that."

Sloane stiffens as their waitress returns to take their orders.

Kay's pointed stare morphs into a warm smile as she looks up at the young woman. "We'll need a few more minutes, thanks."

"Not a problem. Take your time."

The waitress turns. Fizzy water sloshes over the side of Sloane's glass when she sets it onto the table. "That's not your—"

Kay holds up her palm. "I'm not here to judge, dear. I get the sense you know what you're doing."

Her mother-in-law folds her hands atop the table, her large, brilliant cut diamond glistening on her ring finger. "I don't know about you, but I'm starving. That potato gnocchi with pomegranate looks delicious."

Sloane relaxes against her seat. "I think I'll have that too."

Kay orders for them both when their waitress returns. Sloane lets Kay guide the conversation as they wait for their pasta, relieved when Kay turns the topic to her law firm, and the weather in California, not bringing up her and Ethan's marriage again.

"Any word on when you'll be returning to work?" Kay asks, after she finishes telling Sloane how much she loved the latest Reese's Book Club pick.

Sloane nods. "I got a call just an hour ago. I'm cleared to go back starting tomorrow."

"Great news." Kay glances out the window. "You know, it's amazing to me that a man like Brody Carr would show up to the home of a detective's *wife*—a woman he was having an affair with—driving his own car, armed with a gun, and planning to kill her. Not even bothering to check if Ethan was in the house."

Sloane feels a rush of heat rise to her cheeks. Kay sits back in her chair, settling her eyes on Sloane's.

"I don't know what you're getting at." Sloane fights to keep her voice calm. "Brody came over in a rage. He obviously hadn't thought things through."

Kay leans forward. "I just hope that after all you and Ethan have been through, you can *both* find happiness in each other." Her eyes read Sloane's like a book. "A good marriage isn't easy to come by, but it's worth fighting for. As I think you know."

"I've got two orders of our pomegranate potato gnocchi." Their waitress sets their plates in front of them before clasping her hands together. "Can I get you anything else?"

Kay smiles, keeping her focus on Sloane. "I do believe we're all good here. Sloane?"

Sloane unravels her fork from her napkin before setting it on her lap. "Yes. We are."

Chapter 50

The dayshift detectives have all gone home, including Jonah, when Ethan returns to his desk after booking a suspect in the assault case McKinnon gave to him that morning. He checks the time on his laptop after sitting down and sees it's after nine. He should go home, see Sloane before she goes to sleep. There's not much more he can do on his cases tonight anyway. He closes his laptop and stands to put on his coat.

His cell lights up atop his desk with a new email. He glances at the sender: Ricardo Barrera. Not recognizing the name, his eyes move to the subject line: *Kirkland Market security footage*. After the long day he has had, he'd finally managed to push his suspicions of Sloane to the back of his mind.

He pauses after pulling on his coat. Is he really going to dig up her chance encounter with Brody Carr after all they've been through?

He sighs before sitting down and opening his laptop. His heart quickens as he opens the email and clicks on the link to access the video surveillance from the night of his anniversary.

He skims through the different camera viewpoints until he finds the frozen food aisle. Sloane told him she'd gone there to buy his favorite ice cream. After fifteen minutes of fast-forwarding through the footage, he recognizes Sloane's dark hair as she strides down the aisle. She's looking down at her phone with a grocery basket slung over her arm.

Ethan casts a cursory glance at the nightshift detectives on the other side of his cubicle. Both appear to be deeply focused on their computer screens.

Sloane stops in front of the freezer doors and turns to her right before she opens the door. She grabs a pint of ice cream and tosses it into her basket when Ethan spots Brody Carr appear in the edge of the screen. Sloane closes the freezer door and glances at her phone as Carr moves down the aisle, seemingly unaware of her standing there. His head is turned in the opposite direction as his eyes scan the shelves opposite the freezer.

Sloane lifts her head from her phone and stares into the glass. Ethan leans forward in his seat. *What is she doing?* Sloane remains still, her gaze transfixed on the freezer door until Carr walks behind her. He has yet to even look in her direction, his attention still focused on the shelving behind Sloane.

Ethan watches Sloane back up abruptly before pivoting a second before she collides with the startled app founder's chest. A chill runs down his arms when Sloane drops her phone. She waits to reach for it until Carr has already picked it up, placing her hand atop his. Their eyes meet for the first time when they both stand.

Ethan makes a fist with his hand and presses it against his mouth as he watches Carr seemingly recognize Sloane and they appear to chat. He rewinds the footage and presses *play* again. He went back too far, and he stares at the empty aisle waiting for Sloane to appear.

Movement at the end of the aisle catches his eye. Ethan recognizes Sloane walking past the freezer aisle. A man carrying a shopping basket passes by her in the opposite direction. Ethan leans forward, realizing the man is Carr. Sloane turns toward him, who glances in her direction for a split second before looking away. Sloane stops once Carr is out of view. She spins and stares for a moment before following after him.

Ethan swallows, trying to make sense of what he just saw. Despite his wool coat, he feels cold.

After Sloane reappears in the aisle, he turns down the speed of the playback. He watches her look up from her phone and look to the right before opening the freezer door, studying her pointed gaze. She's looking at something or *someone* specific. She opens the freezer door. Seconds later, Carr comes into view.

Ethan pauses the footage. It was Carr she was fixed on before opening the freezer door. He presses *play* and zooms in on Sloane after she tosses the ice cream into her basket. He enlarges the video more until he can tell what Sloane is staring at as she appears to be looking at ice cream. It's Carr's reflection. She waits until he is right behind her before backing straight into him, pivoting into his torso at the last second.

Ethan's thoughts whirl as the video continues to play, capturing their conversation in silence. *Sloane ran into Carr.* Ethan stares at the two of them as Sloane hands her phone to Carr. He closes out of the footage. Sloane *planned* to bump into her college lab partner. There was no question. No accident about it.

Ethan wishes he had access to the FIT case file from their investigation into Brody Carr's death so he could make sure the story Sloane told them was the same she'd told Ethan. He lifts his desk phone and dials the gang unit detective he went to the police academy with, as he continues to scroll through the report, pausing when he finds the case file number from the ballistic match to Carr's gun.

"Gang unit, Detective Pierce."

"Hey, it's Ethan. From homicide."

"You're working late."

"I could say the same for you."

"Yeah, well around here it isn't late until after midnight. What's up?"

"I was wondering if you could email me a case file from 2018. I've got the number right here."

"Sure."

Ethan is met with silence after he reads off the number. He holds his breath, wondering if his old friend recognizes the case from its connection to Carr's killing in Ethan's home.

"I'll send it right over."

Ethan exhales. "Thanks."

It takes less than a minute for the case file to appear in his inbox. Ethan opens the attachment and scrolls through the list of suspects from the unsolved shooting. He knew from the FIT detective who investigated Carr's shooting that she tried to interview the suspects she was able to track down to see if Carr bought the gun off one of them. But none of them were talking. He pulls up his Accurint database and types in the name of the first suspect, along with his date of birth listed in the case file. A red *D* pops on his screen beside the suspect's name, indicating he is deceased. The date of the death is listed as September 6, 2020.

Ethan searches the database for the second suspect, Samuel David Lucas, and another red *D* appears on his screen beside the result. The date of his death was October 27 of this year. Only two days after

Ethan shot Brody Carr in his home. His cause of death is listed as sepsis.

Ethan pulls out his phone and dials the office for the investigators who work for the medical examiner. He glances at the time on his laptop as it rings, knowing his call will probably go to voicemail.

"Investigator Macedo."

Ethan sits forward. "Hey, it's Ethan from homicide."

"Oh! Hey, Ethan, I heard you were back. And evidently working the same hours! Good for you, man. What can I do for you?"

Macedo's warm tone gives no indication that he's holding a grudge or something, like the people in his own office.

"I was wondering if you could give me some information on a death that occurred about a month ago."

"Sure."

"Great. The name of the deceased is Samuel David Lucas, and he died on October 27th."

Ethan hears Macedo's fingertips tap against his keyboard.

"Yep. Got the report right here. There's not much to it. Oh, yeah. I remember this one. I was the one who picked up his body from Bayside. His cause of death was sepsis. IV drug user."

Ethan goes still. "Bayside?"

"Yeah. He'd been in the ICU for a couple of days before we got the call. He was brought to the ER after passing out at a bus stop."

Ethan brings his hand to his temple. If he was brought to the ER two days before he died, it was likely during Sloane's shift.

"There was no next of kin so we—"

"Thanks, Macedo. I gotta run, but I really appreciate your help."

Ethan slams his laptop closed and stands from his chair while slipping his phone into his pocket.

"See ya tomorrow, Marks," one of his coworkers says as he marches out of the homicide unit.

"Good night," Ethan calls over his shoulder.

He throws the door open to the seventh-floor parking area adjacent to the homicide unit, seething with rage as he rushes to his car. Sloane lied about everything. Carr hadn't brought a gun to their home that night. Sloane was so desperate to get rid of Brody Carr that she stole a gun off her patient in the ER.

She planned the whole damn thing.

Chapter 51

Perched on one of her barstools, Sloane smiles at Ethan when he walks into the kitchen. "I have something to tell you. Two things, actually."

He presses his trembling hands against the kitchen island countertop, trying to control the anger seething through his body. He's never been this enraged in his life.

"Like that you lied about Carr bringing a gun to our house? That you actually stole it from a gang member who came into the ER?"

Her face falters, but only for a moment. "How do you know that?"

Ethan recognizes he's more livid now that she's not even bothering to deny it. "Did you lure him over here that night? You must have."

She stares back at him. "Yes."

He takes a deep breath. "Why wasn't there a record of that on his phone?"

"I told him to get a second unregistered phone after you were assigned to Chelsea's case. And I got one too."

Ethan backs away from the counter and paces back and forth, tempted to throw one of Sloane's stupid barstools through the window.

"Only so I could make sure he wasn't going to falsely incriminate me. For a while, I had to pretend like I was on his side."

Ethan grabs a tuft of his hair behind his head and releases it. "Why couldn't you have come forward to Jonah that next morning, like you said you were?" He turns toward her, shocked by the relaxed expression on her face. "You never had any intention of that, did you?"

She purses her lips together. "Brody wasn't ever going to leave me alone. He would've ruined our lives."

Ethan recalls the look in Carr's eyes in his final moments. Sloane screaming at Ethan to shoot. Carr's final words as he swung the pistol toward Ethan, before Ethan silenced him with a bullet to the head. *She's the one.* Carr was trying to defend himself is all.

His jaw falls open. "So, you *killed* him?"

She frowns. "No, Ethan. You did."

A fresh wave of horror flows through his veins.

"You tricked me into believing I was saving your life."

She sighs as if the conversation is irritating her.

Ethan feels his eyes narrow. "You *let* him take the gun from you." He steps toward the island. "You wanted me to shoot him. You *planned* it."

She slides off her barstool. "I knew you would never go along with it if I told you."

Ethan throws his hands in the air. "Because it's *murder!*"

Her face hardens. "It was what needed to be done."

Ethan stares at her in disbelief.

"He was a murderer, Ethan. He killed his wife and used his wealth to prey on young girls and get away with it. He was going to ruin *us*." Sloane moves around the island. "*Us*, Ethan. I did it for *us*. Our marriage."

She reaches for him, but Ethan pulls his arm away.

"You knew it was Brody Carr coming down the aisle at the Kirkland Market on our anniversary. You ran into him on purpose. You planned that, too."

Sloane stiffens. "I had to take action, Ethan. I couldn't stay with you as the poor, pitied wife who got cheated on. We would never have made it if I hadn't done what I did."

"I don't even know you."

He marches past her and storms up the stairs, hearing Sloane trailing behind him when he pulls a suitcase out of the storage closet in the upstairs hallway. After tossing the suitcase onto their bed, he moves to the closet. When he comes out with an armful of clothes, Sloane stands at the edge of their bed, looking between him and the suitcase.

"What are you doing?"

"I'm leaving." He tosses the clothes into the suitcase.

"No, you're not."

"Oh, no?" He takes a step toward her. "What are you going to do? Kill me, too?"

Her lips meld into a hard line. "That's not fair."

He closes the suitcase. "It's not?" The sound of his voice shakes the windows. He's breathing like he needs to escape the room.

"I've been trying to tell you something ever since you came home." She lays a pregnancy test on top of his bag.

Ethan stares at the blue cross in the middle of the stick.

Chapter 52

E than's eyes remain fixed on the pregnancy test for nearly a minute before he lifts his gaze to meet hers. "Is it mine?"

"Of course, it is."

He looks unconvinced.

"I got my period after getting back from the San Juans. It's yours."

"This doesn't change anything."

She watches Ethan sink onto the bed beside his suitcase, knowing that's not true. It changes everything.

"I'm still leaving."

She crosses her arms. "No, Ethan. You're not."

She knows the pain he's felt from having a distant father who always made him feel less than enough. He would never be okay with being around his child only fifty percent of the time. Or less.

"You got what you wanted, Ethan. We're even now. I forgive you, and I need you to forgive me." Her eyes light up as she glances at the pregnancy test atop his bag. "We're going to be a family. Like you always wanted. We can both give our child the things we didn't have growing up. And no one can take that away from us. I've made sure of that."

He clenches his jaw. "Chelsea's toxicology came back positive for oxycodone."

She falls silent. Even though Brody told her he slipped Chelsea the pills, Sloane still hoped it wasn't true.

"You knew she had drugs in her system, didn't you? And you made sure she wouldn't be revived."

She shakes her head. "No!"

She feels a stab of remorse. It wasn't like her to have made an error in judgment as a physician.

"I didn't know." She lowers herself onto the edge of the bed beside him. "You have to believe me."

He turns toward her, his eyes wide with bewilderment. "*Believe you?* After all your lies?" He stands from the bed. "How am I ever supposed to trust you again? I will never know for sure that you didn't have a hand in her death."

She tilts her head back to maintain eye contact with him. "No, you won't. But trust is a choice. It might take time, but it *can* be rebuilt. Remember our therapist?"

"She wasn't talking about *murder,* Sloane!"

No, she was talking about you cheating on me when we were supposed to be trying to have a baby.

Sloane stands as Ethan makes for his suitcase, stopping between him and the bed.

"Move out of my way." His voice is calm this time, but his disdain is evident. "I told you. I don't even know you."

Sloane makes no effort to move. "You've been sleeping in the same bed next to me for nearly a decade, and you're right, you don't even know me well enough to know I'm telling the truth about Chelsea. But whose fault is that? Yours or mine?"

He steps around her. She turns to see him zip his suitcase closed in one angry motion.

"It's yours, Ethan."

He looks up with one hand on his bag. "I'm leaving. Good-bye, Sloane."

Sloane presses her palm against the top of the suitcase. "If you leave, I could tell the police we plotted to kill Brody together. That you helped me lure him to the house, and we staged it to look like self-defense after you shot him."

A shadow moves across Ethan's face. "You'll only incriminate yourself." He keeps his voice steady, but there's no mistaking the trace of terror in his pupils.

She shakes her head. "You're the one who shot him. You had more reason to want Brody dead than I did. He was sleeping with your *wife*. When you found out, you were enraged. And when you found your opportunity to take him out of the picture, you did."

His eyes search hers. "You're not going to turn yourself in for murder."

"That's where you're wrong. You keep underestimating me and look where it's gotten you. I'd rather go to prison than accept less than I deserve. I've come too far in life to fall short now of getting everything I want. The family I never had. It's all or nothing, Ethan. You can stay with me and be happy, or we can go down together." She straightens her posture, daring him to call her bluff.

She studies her husband as he appears to weigh her words. There's an uncertainty in his demeanor now. He knows that he can't predict her anymore.

"You mean stay and be miserable with you?"

She closes the space between them. "You may not love me now, Ethan. But I'm the one for you."

Ethan takes a step back. He snatches his bag off the bed. Sloane braces for him to tell her it's over. That he's never coming back. But instead of making for the door, he drops his suitcase on the floor. Without a word, he grabs his pillow and a blanket off their bed and stalks out of the room, with the bedding tucked beneath his arms.

Moments later, Sloane hears the door to the guest room slam closed. She sinks onto the bed. Relief seeps through her as she places a hand on her belly.

He's not going anywhere. He'll be back in their room, eventually. And he'll never dare to betray her again.

Soon, they'll have the family they both want. Ethan will be the husband and father he desires to be. That she and their child deserve.

What other choice does he have?

Epilogue
Thirty Years Later

Sloane climbs the stairs of her forty-two-foot sailboat, berthed at the Elliot Bay Marina, after stocking the fridge with drinks. Her daughter, Harper, and son-in-law, Jay, will be arriving any minute. Across the Sound, the summer sun glistens against Eagle Harbor. Sloane shades her eyes with her hand to take in Bainbridge Island, where they're heading for dinner.

She hasn't seen Harper since Kay's funeral before the start of the summer. Harper is in the third year of her general surgical residency, working eighty-hour weeks at Bayside. After which, she's hoping to get a fellowship in trauma surgery.

Sloane remembers those days and doesn't envy her daughter. At the moment, Harper's lucky to get a full night's sleep, let alone a social outing.

Harper hasn't spoken of her grandmother since the funeral. But Sloane knows her death was hard on Harper, given how close they were. When Harper attended UCLA as an undergrad, she would make the five-hour drive to stay with Kay on long weekends. And she lived with Kay during her years of med school at UCSF. At ninety-six, Kay was still living on her own—and sharp as a tack—when she died in her sleep.

She stops on the rear deck, thinking of all the good times she's had on this boat, especially when Harper was little. Over the last three decades, sailing had become a constant in her life. She never felt more grounded than when she was out on the water.

She turns to admire her husband as he raises the mainsail on the mast. He catches her staring and grins. She smiles back, thinking he is every bit as handsome at seventy-two as he was when she married him.

A shadow moves across the boat deck in front of her. Sloane turns to see Harper standing on the marina dock, wearing sunglasses and a baseball cap over her long dark hair.

Sloane beams. "Hi, darling."

Harper doesn't return her mother's smile.

Sloane moves toward the railing. "What's wrong?" She scans the empty dock behind her daughter. "Where's Jay?"

"He's not coming." Harper fidgets with her wedding ring, reflecting against the midday sun, before she pushes her sunglasses farther up the bridge of her nose. "We had a fight."

"Oh, honey. I'm sorry." Sloane stretches out her hand as Harper climbs aboard the boat. "Come sit down."

A seagull squawks overhead as Sloane leads her down the narrow set of stairs into the inside cabin.

Harper sits across from her mother at the round dining table. Sloane sees that her eyes are red from crying when she pulls off her sunglasses.

"Hey! Where's my girl?" Ethan's bare feet move slowly down the steps. "I've got our favorite huckleberry ice cream in the freezer."

He stops when she turns toward him. "What's wrong?"

Harper pulls a tissue from her purse and dabs her eyes.

"She and Jay got into a fight," Sloane says.

"I think we're going to get a divorce." Harper sniffs. "Not that you guys could even understand." She sighs. "You've always had the perfect marriage."

Ethan's eyes meet Sloane's. Sloane thinks about how different their marriage was the year before their daughter was born. It took them a few years after everything that happened with Brody before she could describe their marriage as *good*, let alone perfect. But having their daughter bonded them.

By the time they bought the boat, Ethan had started to trust her again. Sloane made sure, as the years went on, not to give him a reason to do otherwise.

She and Ethan started taking sailing lessons after Harper was born, and it quickly became their shared hobby. It was during one of their quiet moments when they were sailing that Ethan opened up about his recent shift in perspective. He didn't like what she did, but he understood that if Sloane hadn't, they would never have made it. They were equals. In no uncertain terms, he also accepted responsibility for his part in the breakdown of their marriage.

When their daughter turned three, they bought the vessel, renaming it *Crystal Seas* after Sloane's mom. It became like a second home to them.

Sloane clears her throat before placing her hand on Harper's forearm. "We had our share of troubles before you were born."

Harper rolls her tear-filled eyes. "Oh, please. Jay and I had more than a scuffle over the cost of some kitchen barstools."

A light flickers in Ethan's eyes. "If you knew how much those barstools cost, you would know it was much more than a *scuffle*."

Harper cracks the faintest of smiles as Sloane watches Ethan continue down the steps. He's always known exactly what to say to lift Harper's spirits on the odd occasion she was feeling down. This was definitely one of them.

"We might understand more than you think," Sloane adds.

Ethan casts Sloane a knowing stare when he takes a seat beside her.

Harper shakes her head. "I doubt it."

Sloane takes her daughter's hand. "Try me."

Acknowledgments

Thanks to my editor, Bryan, for your insight in helping me craft this story and clearing my visibility when things got murky.

Jill, thank you for your guidance over my career and my initial idea for *The One*.

My favorite brother, Cary, thanks for bringing accuracy to the early drafts of my medical scenes from your experience as a paramedic and firefighter.

Rolf, thank you for taking the time to patiently answer my seemingly endless procedural questions for this book, and for reading my final draft.

Kelly, thanks for listening to my fictional scenarios and sharing with me the innerworkings of hospital administration and management.

Tim, thank you for giving me your feedback on this story as both an author and a doctor.

To Jenifer, Penny, and Nancy, thanks for your help in fine-tuning the final draft of this book.

Keira, thank you for all your work behind the scenes.

I am beyond grateful to all the bookstagrammers, bloggers, and readers who have supported my books. Your support means the world to me.

To my college chemistry lab partner, thank you for supporting my writing from the start and holding down the fort many times while I cranked out this story. And to our children, Elise and Anders, thanks for being my littlest and biggest fans. I love you to the moon and back.

Want More?

Get FREE bonus content and new release updates at

AUDREYJCOLE.com/sign-up

About The Author

Audrey J. Cole is a *USA TODAY* bestselling thriller author. She resides in the Pacific Northwest with her family. Before writing full time, she worked as a neonatal intensive care nurse for eleven years.

Connect with Audrey:

 facebook.com/AudreyJCole

 bookbub.com/authors/Audrey-J-Cole

 instagram.com/AudreyJCole

 tiktok.com/@audreyjcole

You can also visit her website:
www.AUDREYJCOLE.com

Printed in the USA
CPSIA information can be obtained
at www.ICGtesting.com
LVHW090905121223
766265LV00044B/933

9 781737 360773